THE LIONHEART'S BRIDE

Berengaria of Navarre
Book One

Austin Hernon

SAPERE
BOOKS

THE
LIONHEART'S
BRIDE

Published by Sapere Books.

24 Trafalgar Road, Ilkley, LS29 8HH

saperebooks.com

ISBN: 978-0-85495-095-9

For my wife, Mandy, curiosity undimmed by years of wandering research, and places as yet unvisited. And my children and grandchildren — read, read, and read again; let no knowledge remain uncovered, nor lessons of history lie unlearned.

PRELUDE

La Réole, Gironde, 2 February 1190

Father Herbert

John, son of Henry II, no longer possessed of any hope of becoming King of England, sat uncomfortably on the edge of the great table. It was set on a plinth at the end of the recently finished great hall of the *maire* in La Réole. He gazed at his brother Richard, King of England — by succession after their father Henry's death, and the scheming of their mother, Eleanor of Aquitaine, who was sitting alongside her newly elevated son.

I was sitting to one side, a candle and a pile of blank parchment on my own small table. I sharpened my quill, ready to record the decisions of this Circus Maximus, for that is what these family gatherings usually turned into. But as Queen Eleanor's confessor, I kept my thoughts to myself.

Richard looked across at me, shifted his muscular frame and growled. 'Write nothing of this, Father Herbert. It is a privy council.'

I laid down my quill and settled back to watch the carnival.

'You've left your visitors waiting outside,' observed John.

'Scroungers,' responded Richard sharply.

I watched the king. He wasn't known for tact. I believed that sometimes he hurt his cause with his rudeness.

'They'll not want for entertainment. Alys is with them,' John added with a snigger.

'Keep quiet, John. That remark is unhelpful,' Eleanor snapped.

'Yes, Mother.'

'This conversation concerns Alys. Let him speak, Mother,' said Richard, but hostile glances were exchanged between the brothers.

'Thank you, Richard. Although Alys was betrothed to Richard —'

'But now she is gone twenty, and no virgin,' interjected John, 'though I'd have expected you to be married by now.'

Eleanor continued unfazed. 'As Alys became the bed companion of your father — while I was held prisoner at Sarum Castle — we need to decide two things. How to deal with the problem of Alys and her brother Philip, and how to manage England while Richard is in Palestine.'

'Marry Alys, and make me Regent. I'll manage England for you ... and Alys, if you want, Richard,' said John.

Richard threw a gauntlet at him, which skimmed his hair. 'There'll be a kicking to follow if you don't mind your manners, brat.'

'Richard, my dear, can we concentrate on the issues? The question of an heir remains.'

Richard's countenance, normally a touch florid, now matched his golden red hair. 'I have a son, madam: Phillip of Cognac thrives.'

'Indeed, Richard, and little heed you pay him. But you need an heir, and Phillip, your bastard, cannot succeed,' replied Eleanor.

'No, but neither will that schemer,' said Richard, staring down at his brother. 'While the Holy Land is beset by foreign warriors, must England also suffer John, Mother? He is unsuited.'

'He is your brother, whom you will depend upon to send you money.'

'And do you not consider yourself, Mother, as Queen Dowager, sufficient to keep a steady hand on the tiller of England?'

'Queen Dowager I shall be, and Regent, while John's hands hover between female flesh and the tiller of England, but I cannot last forever on this earth. You must marry, Richard. You must produce an heir.'

'But I thought that we agreed that Alys is unsuitable.'

'She is, although she was suitable when you and she were betrothed, and you were twelve and she but nine. It was my mistake to leave her at court in England with my reckless husband. But despair not, my son. There is someone whom you have met before and who is quite suitable in all regards: Berengaria of Navarre.'

At the mention of this name, Richard's eyes lit up. This looked hopeful.

'In Pamplona you talked together for some time, as I recall. She seemed quite taken with you.'

'She was … and I remember that she jousted words and jested with me.'

'Will you consider it?' Eleanor pressed.

'I will, Mother. But Philip of France will not be so considerate, I fear. He may demand his sister's dowry back.'

'The domain of the Vexin. Will you yield it?'

'Not a hand-span.'

'Won't he try and take it, Richard? You presume upon your alliance, which is only to Crusade together,' said John, looking for mischief again.

'He'll be too occupied. I might mention it when we are on the way to Jerusalem.'

'This is the plan, my children,' said Eleanor. 'Richard, go to Philip, soften him and then bring up the matter of Alys. We will consult with Archbishop Baldwin of Canterbury on the issue, and I'm certain he'll agree that the young woman is now unsuitable.'

'Archbishops being generally agreeable if their coffers are suitably graced,' added John.

'Then what, Mother?' asked Richard, fondling his second gauntlet.

'We'll send John to govern England —' Eleanor began as Richard's eyebrows met his hairline — 'with William Marshal at his side to guide him.' Richard seemed mollified, so Eleanor continued. 'I'll go to Navarre, to the royal palace in Olite, and conclude the marriage negotiations with King Sancho. I'll bring your bride to you wherever you are, Richard.'

'By faith, madam, your mind is a maze,' exclaimed Richard. 'And I'm free to plan the rest of my Crusade?'

'As you wish, my son, as you wish. But do not bypass Sicily without aiding your sister, Queen Joan. Since the bastard Tancred decided to make a move for the throne after her husband King William died last year, he's been making her life difficult.'

Richard's face reddened, no doubt as he remembered the fate of Joan, the seventh of Henry and Eleanor's brood, although there were many other offspring floating around from Henry's various liaisons.

'I'll go via Sicily, and if my sister has suffered I'll spread my wrath around. Then I'll meet Philip at Vezelay and go on to Marseilles. There I'll gather my invasion fleet and cross over to Sicily.'

'A nice surprise for that Tancred fellow when an invasion fleet turns up on his shores,' said John.

Eleanor confirmed her intentions. 'I'll go to Olite and collect Berengaria, then head for Marseilles. As you will be on your way, so be it — we'll catch up eventually.'

'Are you sure that you can manage such a journey, Mother?' asked John, with false concern.

'If you need to traverse into Italy, the Alpes Maritimes will crumble as you approach, Mother! Not a rock in Christendom would hold up the progress of the Queen Dowager of England, surely?' said Richard.

Eleanor took him by his broad shoulders. 'You may kiss me before you leave.'

Richard bent over the queen and his golden red locks fell over his face as he kissed her hand.

John said naught, but glowered a little. As a priest and scribe, I had watched this family at work for a long time now. I detected a gleam in the eye of the youngest son — John Lackland had spied an opportunity, of that I was certain.

Richard left the chamber and Queen Eleanor caught my eye. Speaking softly, she instructed me, 'I'll see your notes later, Herbert. Prepare yourself to accompany me to Navarre — and beyond if necessary.'

'My lady.' I bowed and escaped as quickly as possible while the events were fresh in my mind.

PART ONE: VIEWS FROM A HORSE

CHAPTER ONE

Palace of Olite, Kingdom of Navarre

Princess Berengaria

I heard Maîtresse Karmele calling for me down the corridor.

'Berengaria, my lady?'

But as I wanted time to think, I kept silent. I was a little troubled. I was now betrothed to the King of England, with his mother on her way to collect me. I was hiding in the corner of my favourite viewing spot, the oriel window in my privy chamber.

The matter of finding me a suitable husband had been left in abeyance for years following my mother's death when I was but twelve years old. I was now well into my twenties, and well past the normal age for such things — but I'd taken on the mantle of king's consort to support my father, Sancho.

I heard a polite cough.

'Who's there?' asked Alazne, one of my waiting ladies.

'Father Ramiro,' came the reply. Our court chaplain stood in the doorway. 'Princess.'

'Father, come in. You seem excited.'

'There is news. Queen Eleanor crossed the border near San Sebastian yesterday, and your father has sent a grand wagon to Pamplona to fetch her. We will be told when she reaches Tafalla, less than an hour away. May I sit a while? I'm going to test you, to see if you are as certain now as when your father proposed this marriage.'

'Must you? Ladies, leave us, please — but Arrosa and Alazne remain, there is something I must ask you.'

My other tending ladies left as bidden.

Father Ramiro sat next to me. 'Will you sit here watching the road for the rest of the day?'

'There is no need,' I said. 'I'm certain that the roads will soon be crowded with couriers, all bursting with news of the queen's progress.'

At that moment, there was another disturbance in the corridor. Ramiro and I looked at each other and laughed.

'Young Sancho!' I said.

'His boots betray his progress,' Ramiro replied.

'I have asked him not to wear them about the palace.'

'You are wasting your breath — he likes to sound important.'

My brother burst into my chamber. 'That woman is on her way,' he declared.

'Good day, Sancho,' I replied. 'Which woman? Maîtresse Karmele, or Eleanor?'

'Both of them. Old Karmele is searching for you, and what are you going do about this Eleanor woman? I've heard that she can be quite demanding.'

'Your sister is good at diplomacy. She averts rather than resists demands,' said Father Ramiro.

'But to become a queen, you need to pay something,' said young Sancho.

'I'll pay my respects to the queen and offer the king something else. I have met him before.'

'Berengaria,' he protested, 'that was thirteen years ago, when you were merely twelve.'

'And he twenty. But he was tall, handsome and wide then. I do not suppose that he has shrunk, nor has he faded from my memory. Perhaps it is no wonder that I have spurned all other

14

suitors, especially when Richard has progressed from Count of Poitou to King of England.'

Maîtresse Karmele bustled into the chamber. 'My lady, I have been searching for you. The Queen of England nears.'

'Indeed, my dear Karmele. Thank you for the news.'

I shooed Ramiro off the window seat and beckoned Karmele, my oldest tending lady, to sit. She had nurtured me all my life and was now struggling a little in mobility. She sat and turned her attention to the road.

Father Ramiro continued to tell me what I already knew — everything having been organised by me — but I let him go on.

'Your Father has organised a banquet for when she arrives, but only for selected guests. King Sancho and Eleanor have agreed to keep your betrothal a secret until King Richard has spoken with King Philip.'

'The King of France will not take kindly to the King of England spurning his sister,' said young Sancho.

'No, but it is rumoured that she has lain with Richard's father and borne him a child,' I said.

'A strange family,' muttered young Sancho. 'Are you certain that you want to involve yourself with them, Berengaria?'

'Only the one,' I laughed. 'I can presume to manage the one. I have sat as queen regent next to Father as good practice.'

'If you keep that woman out of the chamber,' he responded.

'Yes,' Father Ramiro counselled, 'I've heard that Eleanor keeps her nose inside all the bedchambers in her realm.'

'Well, if she thinks that there'll be three in my bedchamber, she can think again.'

'There will be witnesses … to the begetting of Richard's heir,' said young Sancho.

'No! They will need to take Richard's and my assurances for it. I'm not a circus performer.'

My brother laughed. 'I'm off. I'm to rehearse the guard and see if those trumpeters have their notes right, although I can't tell the difference myself.' He left, his footsteps echoing down the corridors.

'Well,' said Father Ramiro, 'that was a little near the bone.'

'Dear Father, we are both well experienced in the ways of the world, so worry not for me,' I said. 'If my duty is to grow an heir to the kingdom of England within me, then so be it. Should you go and see if there is more news?'

The priest nodded and exited the chamber.

I beckoned to my remaining ladies. 'Alazne and Arrosa, I must choose some gowns if I am to chase through Europe after my husband-to-be — and I have something to ask of you. Will you come with me, attend me wherever we go?'

'Ooh!' exclaimed Arrosa, clapping her hands. 'To England?'

I realised that she had not understood the full meaning of Eleanor's visit. 'No, dearest, to the Holy Land, if needed. Richard is on his way to Marseilles to take ship, and we must catch up with him before I can marry him.'

Alazne smiled. 'I'll come, I'll go with you to the ends of the earth, Your Highness.'

'Of course,' added Arrosa. 'I'm coming too.'

'And me,' said Karmele. 'I'll go to Jerusalem to be shriven.'

That was a surprise, but the prize of eternal salvation in return for a pilgrimage was a magnificent reward, so how could I refuse?

I heard young Sancho's voice ringing loudly across the receiving chamber as we progressed along the corridor.

'Is Berengaria not ready yet? Where are Blanca, Constance and Theresa? They must have finished preparing their sister by now.'

'Patience, Prince Sancho,' Father Ramiro responded. 'Queen Eleanor must have time to rest after her journey. We will be told when she is ready to leave the guest chamber, then our Princess Berengaria will be seated ready to greet her.'

'This has the makings of a joust,' growled King Sancho.

I made my way to my throne between the bowing courtiers, and my father looked round.

'Ah, daughter, you heard us?'

'Yes. I will prepare to receive the Queen Dowager of England as a present princess and a future queen. I have great respect for Eleanor, famed throughout Europe as she is, but I will be nobody's pawn. I see, Father, that you have provided a throne for her alongside yours.'

'Indeed, as befits her station. It is the height of your own, fear not; you will not be diminished in that regard.'

I pondered as we awaited her arrival. Kings, queens, princesses — a very odd confluence for a tiny land such as Navarre.

Then King Sancho, on a nod from the domo by the grand entrance, bade young Sancho take his place behind his throne, set near the grand marble fireplace. My brother moved silently, bereft of weaponry for once, and stood behind our father and me. Selected courtiers gathered at a respectful distance in a semicircle.

Then trumpets blasted, heralding the arrival of Eleanor. There was a gasp from the audience as she entered, the most powerful woman in Europe, her two attending ladies a couple of steps behind her. Then, with her eyes settling upon her hosts, she smiled and the room lit up. Tall and elegant, she was dressed in an embroidered golden robe.

Everyone bowed as King Sancho stepped forward to greet his royal guest.

'King Sancho, we meet once more,' Queen Eleanor exclaimed.

'Indeed we do, gracious queen,' he replied. He offered his hand and she took it in both of hers.

I stood and followed my father, and Eleanor turned to me.

'Berengaria,' she said, smiling, 'a bud blossomed since we last met. Come, embrace your future mother-by-law.' She clasped me to her bosom.

'My daughter has grown in experience and wisdom, Eleanor, and has been my rock for these past years since my beloved wife, Sancha died.'

Eleanor's eyes softened as she moved back to hold my gaze. She then turned me so that we were both facing Father. 'Sancho, I value wisdom above all, and given your reputation it is no surprise that your daughter has inherited such qualities.' Pulling me close, she continued, 'I am pleased to meet you again, Berengaria.'

She held my hand as she allowed herself to be conducted towards the throne by my father to meet Prince Sancho.

My brother grinned down at her. 'Queen Eleanor, a pleasure to meet you, an honour indeed.' He gave a small bow to honour her but made no attempt to treat her as anything but an equal — after all, she needed this alliance as much as Father.

Eleanor headed towards my throne, but Father skilfully turned her towards her intended seat.

I struggled to settle in my throne in my heavy skirts. Alazne and Arrosa stepped forward to help and then take their position behind me.

Leaning forward, Eleanor said, 'You are such a vision, Berengaria, and I can see that you are now most comely. Richard should consider himself graced by you. Come, let me greet you properly.'

Evidently she did not like the idea of King Sancho's throne coming between us, so she stood and beckoned me forward so that we could embrace.

'My lady,' I said sweetly, returning her gaze.

'And now I can ask you directly what you think of a marriage to my son, Richard. Are you willing, Berengaria?'

'I am indeed, my lady. Ever since we met, he has been in my mind. God has planned this, I am certain.'

'All these years, my child? Such dreams, such steadfastness.' Turning to Father, she smiled and said, 'It seems that my prayers and Berengaria's dreams are one and the same. What say you, Sancho, is there to be a wedding?'

'It would seem so, Eleanor. If you are happy to join our families together, then it will suit me well.'

My father stood, and we closed in to form a royal group, engaged in a conversation about weddings. Father Ramiro gave a signal to the domo, and the air was filled with sweet music. The guests drifted into the adjoining *aretoa* and were soon happily dancing.

My father cleared his throat as he raised a difficult question. 'Eleanor, have Richard and Philip agreed to end the engagement between Richard and Alys?'

'As I understand it, Sancho, the two kings have agreed to discuss the issue when they meet, which will be soon, as they are both headed for the coast at Marseilles. As far as Richard is concerned, he has no intention of marrying his father's cast-offs.'

I was not certain that a princess of France could be got rid of so easily. But there was time to remove that obstacle, and with no further discussion invited, Eleanor turned the conversation to the preparations necessary for a winter journey down to Marseilles.

Once we had agreed on the plans, she grasped me by the shoulders and spoke gently into my ear. '*Thinking* of marrying the King of England and *doing* it are two different things. Are you brave? You will be very far from home, Berengaria, and you will find this crown an uncomfortable weight.'

There was a sudden start in my heart, but I collected myself. 'If it suits *us*, Your Highness, I'll make a good try of it.'

She stared at me. 'Well, well, I see that you have a will. You should know that Richard's will has developed into a well-honed barb now that he is king. Think not that you can tame him, although it seems that you have been in his thoughts for a number of years.'

'Yes, Your Highness, there are some things which we will need to discuss. I'm sure that if we are of a like mind, your son and I will fulfil this proposal.' I maintained a steady gaze, being careful not to show any dissent at this stage, but if she persisted in trying to dominate me, she would find any prospect of friendship disappearing.

The challenge must have been observed by Father, who intervened quickly. 'How was your journey from Pamplona, Eleanor? Was the wagon to your liking?'

'Indeed it was, Sancho. A splendid wagon in every way fit for a queen.'

'Indeed, and will you take it for your onward journey?'

'Oh no, Sancho. I have a special wagon for my use. I took yours for the final part of my journey, but I will go onwards in mine. Is it not intended for Berengaria?'

'I prefer to ride,' I said, 'although the wagon can be brought along, in case I'd like a change of view.'

'I'm sure that we can travel together from time to time and have some interesting conversations along the way. However, for tonight perhaps you will excuse me if I retire a little early. I am somewhat weary from the journey, and my crown is heavy.' She turned to my father. 'If I could take some refreshment in my chambers?'

'All will be arranged, Eleanor. Please allow me to escort you to your chambers. How many tending ladies do you have with you? Perhaps we can discuss the travel arrangements in the morning and —'

'We will be leaving in the morning, Sancho. The weather can quickly turn against one at this time of year — there is no time to lose.'

Their voices faded as they both left the chamber, leaving me standing. My brother came across and put an arm around my shoulder.

'I think that she likes you. I have heard she leaves people whom she does not like shrivelled up when she makes her departure. But you made a good point when you indicated that you intend to travel independently.'

'I can see a most interesting journey in the offing. Take me to my chambers; I must prepare my ladies. Have you decided who will be the captain of my escort yet?'

'Indeed, your favourite. It will be Captain Javier, your riding master.'

'Good, at least that's a comfort. And my horse?'

'Your favourite Arabian palfreys — three of them to see you safely to wherever it is you are off to.'

'And wagons for my wardrobe?'

'Ah! I have a surprise for you. We have had a look inside the queen's wagon, and another that her escort brought. This one is fitted out as a travelling bedchamber. It has a bed and hanging devices for clothes ... and a space for, erm, relieving oneself.'

I giggled at the thought. 'A travelling *aseo*? How thoughtful.'

'Indeed. One of your wagons is being worked upon to match that as we speak; you will not lack facilities. How are your ladies travelling?'

'Alazne will ride with me. Arrosa, poor girl, is not enamoured of horses, so I suppose that she will travel by wagon with Karmele. Will there be room on the driving seat of my new itinerant *aseo*?'

'Of course — the bench is well padded. It will need to be, for that long journey.'

'Indeed, and I'll have a full escort?'

'Yes, twenty-five of our best men.'

'How many does Eleanor have?'

'Thirty.'

'And my twenty-five is a diplomatic number, Sancho?'

'Sometimes I can be diplomatic. Come here, let me hold you. I worry for you. Father Ramiro is sending Father Petri as your confessor.'

'Petri! But he is a miserable man, always on his knees.'

'Exactly. He will not bother you much. You only need to use him when you have need.'

CHAPTER TWO

I did not see Eleanor again until I spilled out of my quarters and into the palace yard the following day. It was chaos. Young Sancho dashed up the steps to greet me.

'See this, Berengaria, the whole town has turned out to see you off. We left you sleeping. I came into your chamber while Alazne and Arrosa were still busy sending your clothes down to pack into your wagon.'

'I must thank them. Where is Eleanor?'

'Down by the palace yard gate. There is her travelling wagon, see. She is climbing in now.'

Eleanor's wagon had large wheels and a hood, with two splendid horses harnessed in tandem to pull it — the like of which I had not seen before.

'Where did that come from?' I asked.

'She left it in San Sebastian to arrive in the royal wagon we sent for her at the border. It is well appointed, with cushions and the like. I've heard from her escort captain that there are more wagons waiting at the border. You are to go to the coast at San Sebastian, skirt around the northern edge of the Pyrenees into Aquitaine, then head for Toulouse and then Marseilles.'

'No surprises there. She will not travel through Aragon?'

'No, certainly not. Remember the purpose of your marriage is to place Navarre as a buffer between her lands in Aquitaine, and Castile and Aragon; Father is playing a clever game.'

'I know. This is not so much a marriage of love as one of diplomatic convenience. It's for the safety of our kingdom.'

My brother took me by the shoulders. 'You are very brave, Berengaria, and I love you very much. I will pray for you every day.'

'And I for you, but worry not. This is an adventure. I might get to see the Holy Land! Think what that will do for my soul.'

After a while, Father came to us. 'Come now, daughter,' he said. 'I would speak to Eleanor before she departs.'

The crowds parted as we made our way towards Eleanor's wagon, although they did not cease to wave the flags of Navarre and Aquitaine.

'Sancho!' Eleanor exclaimed as we came up to her. She was almost hidden by furs in her wagon. Looking down, she observed me closely. 'You are well dressed, my dear ... but not for a wagon ride.'

I was dressed in breeches, a split doeskin kirtle, a satin undershirt, a thick woollen shirt and over that a quilted gambeson to keep out the cold as we climbed into the mountains. A cloak with a splendid fur hood completed the ensemble.

'I shall be riding, Your Highness,' I told Eleanor. 'I have my string of Arabians to carry me whither ... I know not.'

'She has been riding since she could walk, Eleanor,' my father added. 'A splendid saddle she sits, I must tell you.'

'Does she now? Well, that's as may be. Do you think that you could join me now and then in this splendid wagon? There's room for two, and we can have a little talk.'

'It would be my pleasure, Your Highness. It will ease my horse's load a little.'

'And your backside, no doubt.'

Father chortled at that remark. Perhaps Eleanor had a sense of humour after all.

'Well,' he said, 'I suppose if you're going, you might as well be about it.' So saying, he enveloped me in another bear hug. He then put his hands up to Eleanor and she grasped them firmly.

'Worry not, wise Sancho, she will want for nothing and we will keep her safe. I look forward to the day when our kingdoms are united against all who would threaten us. Farewell and God bless you.'

'Farewell, my good lady; my regards. Carry my blessing to your son, Richard.'

With that, we stepped back and Eleanor waved an imperious hand, whereupon the captain of her guard shouted to a groom perched atop the second horse and the whole contraption lurched forward, leading the royal caravan.

I walked back to where my horse was waiting, everyone else being in position, and climbed onto her back using Father's knee as a springboard. I was accompanied by Alazne on horseback and Arrosa and Karmele in our wagon.

The mood was jolly and the crowd began to call out to me, wishing me well and praying for my safe return. Smiling and waving, we wound our way through the town until all fell silent, save for the noise of this splendid cavalcade.

I could not help but turn at the last house on the road and gaze back at the turrets of the palace, the place where I had spent the happiest days of my life so far.

I had been occupied with my thoughts for a while when Javier, the captain of my guards, pulled alongside me.

'Your Highness, are you settled?' he asked. 'There's quite a way to go.'

'Indeed, Javier. And now you can relate to me how we are going to set about it. I confess that I have not given as much thought to the matter as I should.'

'Of course. Ahead, with her close escort, is Queen Eleanor, as you know. Beyond her are some important people; you may catch a glimpse of them now and then. Miles ahead are the scouts; they will be on the lookout for danger, and also escorting two kitchen wagons.'

'Kitchen wagons?'

'Indeed. One wagon will be far in advance with its own escort, and when it reaches a predetermined spot, the crew will stop and prepare the evening meal for this whole cavalcade.'

'Clever. And the second wagon?'

'It will have already gone much further ahead to reach the place for the second evening.'

'It is travelling a day ahead of us?'

'Correct. The kitchen crews will have a day free from time to time, because in various locations Queen Eleanor expects to find hospitality in the grand houses we will encounter along the way.'

'That sounds interesting. Where will the first such place be, Javier?'

He laughed. 'You know it: the palace at Pamplona — *your* palace.'

I laughed along with him. 'Of course, one day's journey. Is that the pattern of it then, twenty to twenty-five miles per day?'

'Depending on the terrain and the gradients.'

I fell silent at that, until Alazne piped up from behind.

'When will we reach Marseilles, Captain Javier?'

'In a month, after Christmas.'

I had one night in a familiar bed in Pamplona, a night under the stars in my wagon, and then a night in a draughty castle overlooking San Sebastian's fine bay, before we turned north and entered Eleanor's Aquitaine.

When we began our climb into the northern Pyrenees, I was summoned to join Eleanor. Captain Javier led me to her.

Eleanor's accommodation wagon was halted at the head of her escort and she was taking a little walk by the side of the track.

'Ah, there you are, Princess Berengaria. There seems to be a stretch of level track in front of us — would you care to walk a little? I find that my bones seize up if I sit in the wagon for too long.'

We set off and the wagons trundled along behind. I could hear the creaking of Javier's leather as well as the harnesses of Eleanor's close guard, which never strayed far from her.

'A fine view from up here,' she offered as an opening. 'Do you know what the scenery is like in the Holy Lands? I have heard tales from pilgrims. They tell of arid lands with little water, save in the winter, of course, when it can rain a lot.'

'Really? That is surprising.'

'It may be the first of many surprises awaiting you. But you are an adventurous young woman, or so I've heard.'

'True, I like trying new things, Your Highness.'

'Men? How about men?'

'No, I have avoided that.'

She stopped and fixed me with a penetrating gaze. 'You have some idea of what marriage is about, I presume?'

'Lying together? I breed horses. I supposed it to be similar with men.'

Eleanor laughed. 'I suppose so. I had many children with Henry, but he had an appetite beyond what I could offer.'

Henry's peccadillos were well known in court circles, but I was surprised that she was so open about it. Perhaps she was too old to care.

'You have confirmed that Richard has repudiated his fiancée, Alys?'

'Yes, he's not going to follow his father into that valley.'

'Am I merely a substitute for her?'

'No, dear girl, you are not. When we realised that you were still available, Richard jumped at the chance. If it were not for this Crusade, he would be by your side even now. You are prepared to conceive an heir?'

'I'll manage. I do have a certain curiosity, even if I lack the practice of it.'

'Then I'm certain that Richard will indulge your curiosity to your satisfaction. Here is the end of this level ground. If you help me back into my wagon, we'll move on a bit further. Soon we'll be out of Aquitaine and into the county of Toulouse, where we'll be assured of a welcome, as pilgrims. I expect there'll be a nice bed in Château Narbonnais in Toulouse town for you. Such a pleasant change for a night or two, don't you think?'

'Indeed, Your Highness,' I said as I helped her climb into her wagon.

She was soon ensconced, and her ladies, Adelaide and Corinne, threw furs over her.

Ten days after setting out, we were toiling and breathless in the heights of Tarbes an ancient town that had once been home to the Romans; then it was downhill towards Toulouse. We had settled into a routine governed by the short December days, although now that we had the mountains behind us, we could mostly manage twenty-five miles per day. It was a breathtaking pace for a well-drilled company, which I now knew totalled over one hundred persons of various crafts and skills.

CHAPTER THREE

We arrived at Château Narbonnais in Toulouse after sixteen days. The courtyard was heaving, and my contingent merely added to the confusion. It was difficult to tell the inhabitants from the townsfolk, who it seemed had all turned out to greet us. Some imperious fellow pushed his way through the throng to hold the bridle of my horse.

'Princess Berengaria, allow me to introduce myself. I am Count Raymond. I am pleased to welcome you to Château Narbonnais, and I apologise for this unruly mob. If you come with me, I'll conduct you safely to the great hall.'

Count Raymond, a man in his fifties, I guessed, helped me down from the saddle.

'You need not apologise for such a jolly crowd, Count Raymond,' I said. 'They have made us most welcome. May we wait a moment? My ladies are somewhere in this melee.'

Once they were located, I asked to be taken to my quarters for the night. Raymond was very gracious and made no fuss. I fell into bed and was asleep almost immediately.

The next moment, I was awoken by Alazne's soft voice in my ear. 'Time to go, Princess. Everyone else has left.'

'How rude,' I said.

By the time I attended the great hall, there were only my people left.

'Eleanor was eager to set off,' Count Raymond informed us. 'She had a hamper of food and said she would eat along the way. She's keen to catch up with Richard.'

'If he's still there to be caught up with,' I said.

When I was finally mounted and ready to set off, I told Alazne, Arrosa and Karmele to go on ahead. 'I want to talk to Father Petri. I'll catch up later.'

They left with puzzled expressions.

I found my confessor sitting on one of the baggage wagons, his donkey abandoned. I startled him as he came past, causing him to nearly topple off the bouncing bench.

'Good day, Father Petri,' I greeted. 'We have not had an opportunity to talk much so far. May I ride with you?'

'Oh! Oh, Princess Berengaria. I was praying — excuse me, I did not see you. Yes, yes, it is quite pleasant, and this dry weather is helping us along with God's blessing.'

We fell silent for a while, watching the countryside go by.

'I like the sea,' I said. 'I like Pamplona, but I like to visit San Sebastian and watch the fishermen there.'

'Indeed,' responded Father Petri, 'and Christ was a fisherman of souls, of course.'

'He was, and he loved the catchers of fish for what they did.'

'He loved all men … and women,' added the priest.

'Women? Are women different, Father?'

He looked at me oddly. Perhaps I had offended him. 'They are, in many ways.'

'But should they be loved?'

'Of course, why do you say that? Did not Jesus love his mother Mary? He would not have come among us without her. And Mary Magdalene, he loved her too. All souls are valuable in the eyes of Jesus.'

'He saved women who had strayed too,' I added.

'He did, and he forgave them their trespasses.'

I settled down to contemplate this: all souls were valuable, and all souls were to be loved.

We stopped just then for refreshment. Father Petri, not one to miss an opportunity, gathered us together to pray. I seemed to have set him thinking, because he manged to fit in a sermon that concentrated on love and kindliness.

When we set off again, I stayed in front of the wagons with the sergeant of the escort. Those in the caravan in front of us had got so far ahead that the piles of horse droppings had ceased to steam as we passed them by. We arrived at Eleanor's camp just as it was turning dark.

'Just in time for the evening meal,' laughed Alazne as she helped me down. She planted a kiss on my cheek and held my wrist a little longer than necessary before a gentle cough from Arrosa parted us.

'Queen Eleanor is taking advantage of the weather and has erected a marquee to banquet within tonight. We are expected soon, Princess.'

'How kind. She is well organised, I must say. I don't think that I will be wearing one of my best gowns, though. This morning's walking apparel is suitable, do you agree?'

'We agree,' the pair chorused. We had time to change my clothing and tidy my hair before trooping off to find Eleanor. Karmele elected to retire instead of attending with us.

Eleanor had changed into a resplendent gown, worthy of Raymond's court if not that of the Pope himself. I went up to her table and received an imperious wave, indicating that I should sit next to her. I took my place and began to address the platters laid out in front of me.

'I trust that you will not be late for your wedding, Berengaria.'

'If we ever catch up with my betrothed, I shall try not to be.'

She sniffed and said naught for a while. Then she went on, 'We shall have better accommodation at Carcassonne tomorrow and Narbonne two days after that. They have been informed of my coming.'

'Is that because we are pilgrims, Your Highness, or because you are the Queen of England?'

She laughed. 'Both, I suspect. Perhaps one day doors will open for you in the same way,' she said with a glint in her eye.

The meal ended when Eleanor clapped her hands and announced that she was off to bed. I stood up to see her off and then beckoned Arrosa and Alazne to join me at Eleanor's table.

We talked for a while before leaving to find my wagon in the dark. It was illuminated by a brazier at the rear, and two soldiers were warming their hands alongside.

'Captain Javier has chosen us to guard you, Your Highness,' said one cheerfully.

'Why, thank you. I'm certain that we shall be quite safe with you here. Goodnight and God bless.'

'Here are candles to light your way. Make sure that you blow them out before you go to sleep. Goodnight, Your Highness.'

Climbing into the wagon, I made my way to the far end, where my bed beckoned. The berths for Karmele, Alazne and Arrosa were along the sides. One of the berths was already occupied by Karmele; I heard her snoring on my way to the front. My section was curtained off and quite private, and there was a double skin of canvas over it to keep it warm.

For now, I didn't draw the curtain. Alazne sat down on her bed and began to take off her outer garments, leaving Arrosa to attend me.

'That was a nice evening, Arrosa, but what do you make of Eleanor? I can't work out her actions, I'm sure.'

'Neither can I. Perhaps we should wait a while before passing judgement. Do you think that we'll ever catch up with her son, Princess?'

'No son, no marriage. If he wants an heir, he'd better stand still for a while.'

Waking gently, I heard Arrosa coughing discreetly on the other side of the curtain.

'Everybody's up, Princess,' she said. She drew back the curtain and found me struggling to pull my silk nether breeches on. 'There's not a lot of room in here, Princess. Stand up and I'll help you dress.'

I did as I was bidden, wondering whether a strange château was better than a familiar wagon. 'Where's Alazne?'

'Gone to find some food — ah, that'll be her now,' Arrosa said as Alazne came in. She pushed a wicker basket full of food, topped by a flagon of wine, onto the bed.

'There's enough there for us all, Princess.'

'And me?' Karmele was awake now.

After we were all dressed for the day, the contents of the basket and the flagon soon disappeared.

'I'll clear out of your way and see to the horses,' I said, leaving them to tidy up.

That night, we were to be accommodated in the Château Carcassonne, which turned out to be an enormous citadel.

We were greeted by Count Raymond's son, Raymond-Roger. He was a pleasant fellow, but I could not delay asking where my bedchamber was.

Eleanor sniffed at my request. 'Do try and be on time in the morning, Berengaria. We have much further to travel.'

When she had swept through the doorway, Raymond-Roger turned to me and said, 'Follow me, Your Highness, and we'll get you settled.'

As soon as it was polite, I thanked him and he left, wishing me a sound sleep.

The corridor was still quite busy. Eleanor, whose chamber was across the way, was having some kind of dress crisis with her ladies. I lay in my bed, trying to decide how I should deal with her.

The next morning, after Prime and breakfast, I was back on my horse. We spent the day travelling through the countryside and then once again slept in our wagon.

While mounting my horse the following day, I asked Javier about our next destination, Narbonne.

'The town is on the Roman Via Domitia and is an old Roman port,' he said. 'It is where the river Aude meets the Mare Nostrum, across which lies the Holy Land — our destination, I believe.'

I blinked; I had expected to meet and marry Richard in Marseilles.

'Perhaps you should discuss it with the queen, Your Highness,' added Javier.

'Perhaps I should,' I replied. 'Thank you, Captain. Please attend to your duties.'

That night we had cold meats, eggs and bread at the roadside, with all the wagons pulled up close and the horses tethered together nearby. The air was milder now that we were near the sea. We were surrounded by vineyards, and so we had access to wine. After more than a sip of that, I felt emboldened enough to go and find Eleanor.

'Come with me, Karmele,' I said. 'I want to know how far I'm expected to go, following her son. She might not trust me enough to tell me that her son may have left Marseilles by the time we get there. Perhaps she is concerned that I would not pursue Richard all the way to Jerusalem.'

Finding Eleanor's wagon wasn't difficult. It was lit up like a church, with candles and braziers in full flame. She was sitting in a chair, covered with furs, and had some minstrels playing nearby.

I coughed and she beckoned me forward, Karmele clinging to my hand.

'Come for some food, Berengaria? You two look anxious.'

'No, Your Highness, we've eaten.'

'What is it, then? I'm about to go to bed, but I can wait, especially for my intended daughter-by-law.'

'Are we going to cross the sea if … if the king has left Marseilles when we get there?'

'Oh! Did I not inform you? His fleet is still assembling at Marseilles and will move on to Sicily, where we will join him. Did you not know that he intends to visit his sister Joan?'

'No, Your Highness. Why would he do that?'

'Because since her husband died, some usurper has taken his place, stolen her dowry and put her in confinement. Richard intends to reverse all those wrongs.'

'I did not know that. Where will we go, if Richard has gone to Sicily?'

'There will be a ship waiting for us at Marseilles, do not fret. And we could also ride through Italy to the Strait of Messina. I'm not too fond of the sea.'

'Italy?' I repeated.

'Yes, Berengaria, Italy. You know where that is, surely?'

'I do, Your Highness. Thank you for your help. Goodnight.'
I'd had enough of her.

'Goodnight ... daughter.'

I left with my cheeks burning, still holding Karmele's hand.
'If Eleanor's son has developed his mother's manners since last
I met him, then she can find a brood mare elsewhere,' I told
her. 'I'll not suffer more of this.'

After a restless night, we were on our way as dawn broke. The
days were at their shortest, so it was almost dark by the time
we reached Narbonne. The harbour was a huge inlet, fed by
the sea but with the river Aude running into it.

Javier approached me. 'Your Highness, there may be a
problem. Viscountess Ermengarde is not here. She is resting at
Abbaye de Fontfroide, some miles away, and the castellan,
Captain André, has informed me that they have limited
quarters for visitors. There is only a simple donjon, and the
queen has taken the only bedchamber. Would you mind
remaining in your wagon tonight?'

'No, if needs must, Javier. After all, we are pilgrims. Should
we not suffer a little along the way?'

'You are very brave, Your Highness. I'll set up the camp
outside the donjon and see to some food.'

'Thank you. See if you can send someone along with a carafe
of that local wine; it is quite palatable.'

I was pleased when the tents were erected, especially the
komunak tent — the place where we relieved ourselves. The
camp steward brought a smile to my face when he turned up
and announced, 'We have set up the *komunak* in those trees
over there, Your Highness, and a canvas screen down by the
water's edge. If you would like to make use of it, the water is
not too cold, but if you care to wait, I have a cauldron on the

fire for some hot water. Oh, and I have two carafes of wine and some goblets.'

'Thank you, how thoughtful. Ladies, the sea beckons. Let's rid ourselves of the odours of the journey. Arrosa, bring some fresh clothes from the wagon; I sense a new beginning in the morning. This is the last stop before we reach Marseilles.'

Sitting on the sand, Alazne and I pulled each other's boots off and undressed. The water was not welcoming at first, but my body warmed as I went out a bit further.

Turning, I watched as Alazne followed me, her body lit by the moon. She was lithe and beautiful as she splashed about.   ·

When we returned to our wagon, the steward was waiting with our food and wine. Alazne, Arrosa and I managed to finish two carafes between us.

A banging on the back of the wagon gave us a rude awakening, and I was pushed onto the back of my horse before I had begun to focus properly. I ate nothing all morning, and we were making our way along the Via Domitia before I took much heed of anything. Alazne rode by my side.

'Is Arrosa on the front seat of the wagon?' I asked her blearily.

Alazne looked behind. 'Yes, she seems disgustingly healthy. She is beaming and conversing with her postilion.'

'I'm not having any more wine.'

'Very wise, Princess.'

By noon I was feeling better, and we came to a halt beside our itinerant kitchen.

Javier came over and helped me down. 'A little wine and cheese might bring a smile to your face, Your Highness. You seem a little down today. Anything I can do to help?'

'No,' I replied, before running into a nearby thicket to throw up.

I took a little wine and felt better for it, and I took a bag with some bread and cheese with me on my horse. By nightfall I was feeling much better, but I slept early after nibbling some fruit.

I enjoyed the next five days as we skirted town after town. Eleanor was setting a spirited pace, and we did not see each other as she was always ahead. Some days we managed nearly thirty miles, and the soldiers began to worry about their steeds. Captain Javier ordered that only those out on patrol would wear their chainmail; the others could remove it and place it in a wagon to save the horses some effort. A week after leaving Narbonne, Marseilles came into view late one morning.

'I can't see many ships, Princess,' said Alazne anxiously.

'No, neither can I. Captain Javier, go forward and find Queen Eleanor. See what's happening.'

'Of course, Your Highness. We might be riding on to Italy by the looks of things, unless there's a vessel hidden somewhere.'

He was gone for a long time, and when he returned he looked worried.

'How much do you know about King Richard's intended journey, Your Highness?'

'Eleanor said that he might have gone on to Sicily, but we could expect a ship to follow him in from here. Have you seen her? Do you know something?'

'I've heard that Richard left here two weeks ago, and the rest of his fleet followed a few days later. He crossed the Strait of Messina to Sicily on the twenty-second of October — there never was a suitable ship left here for you.'

'And Eleanor knew this?' piped up Alazne.

'I have a reliable source that says she did. We are to dash down through Italy to take a ship to Sicily from the south. It is intended that you marry in Sicily in Queen Joan's realm — after Richard has reclaimed it from the usurper king, Tancred.'

'Where is Eleanor now?'

'At the harbour. There is one fast galley waiting there; I believe that it will be used to carry messages between her and Richard as she travels through Italy.'

'We will go there immediately, Javier. I will face Eleanor and see what she has to say. I will play a part in this mummery, whether she likes it or not.'

Karmele looked worried. 'Your Highness, please give yourself time to consider this — all may not be as it seems. You could risk everything by charging at Eleanor like this.'

I placed an arm around Karmele's shoulders. 'Worry not, I'll be gentle. Alazne, on your horse; Arrosa, see to the wagon and follow us down to the waterside. Now, let's set off, Captain.'

I wanted to catch Eleanor and her clandestine galley together, and I thought I might send a message to my betrothed myself.

CHAPTER FOUR

We arrived at the quayside in time to watch a galley speed out to sea. Eleanor was watching but turned to face me when I reined in.

'Ah, Berengaria, if you had been here earlier, you might have sent a message to Richard, see —' she pointed at the flashing oars of the boat — 'it is off to Sicily.'

'Yes, Your Highness. It's one of the disadvantages of following along behind: I tend to arrive after you.'

'Indeed. Perhaps you can attend me more often. I'm not certain why you are trailing in my wake, but if you could come to me each day, we can discuss matters more thoroughly.'

'Much time is spent avoiding piles of horse ordure, Your Highness. Perhaps I could come forward each evening and you can explain your plans. And if there happens to be a spare galley thereabouts, perhaps I could send a message to my betrothed. As for now, why this pointless gallop to Marseilles? The horses are in need of rest, and it has served no purpose.'

'Oh, my dear, it has a purpose. If there are no ships left behind that are suitable to contain our whole cavalcade, we must cross over into Italy via the Alpes Maritimes, and the snows may not be far off.'

'Christmas must be near — I had forgotten that. We have come so far.'

'Are you eager to meet your future husband? That would tend to distract the mind. If you can attend me each day, we will remind you of our intentions, and of course, if there is an opportunity you can send messages to Richard. We will be having prayers tomorrow at the church of Blessed Mary.

Bishop Ranier is to conduct the service, and we will be pleased to see you at a reception in his palace afterwards. Do you agree?'

'Thank you, Your Highness. We are for certain to ride into Italy?'

'Indeed. Richard was to call at Genova; no doubt he will have left news of his intentions. Do you think that you can find a suitable gown for the morning?' she asked, looking at my riding attire.

'Of course. Is that all?'

'Indeed, until tomorrow. God bless you, my dear.'

Once out of earshot, I gave way to my frustration. 'Who does she think she is?' I growled.

'You'll need to plan better, Princess,' said Alazne. 'She is ahead of you.'

The following day dawned bright and cool. I called out from behind my curtain as I drew on my nether breeches.

'A joyful day to you, my ladies!'

'God's blessing to you, Princess!' Alazne responded.

'Have you retrieved a gown from the chests, Alazne? I must appear resplendent.'

'You are to appear *appropriate*, Your Highness, as a princess or a queen should,' replied Karmele.

I stood up and drew back the curtain. The steward, who was placing some food on the back of the wagon, nearly dropped his tray as he was treated to a full view of the royal nether garments.

'Princess!' shrieked Karmele, scandalised, as Alazne and Arrosa burst into laughter. The steward quickly disappeared.

'It is nothing he has not seen before, I'm sure. Where is my gown?'

Alazne and Arrosa were clutching a long blue kirtle and a white shirt. Alazne was also holding a white mantilla and my princess's coronet.

'Are you sure? I'll look like those statues of Mary,' I said, crossing myself.

'You can't get more pious than that, Princess,' said Alazne.

'You devils! How much time have we got?'

'Not a lot, and Captain Javier has found you a lady's saddle, so you need to get used to that.'

'A lady's saddle? Oh no, you don't mean…'

'It's in favour in the best courts in Europe.'

'Is this your idea of a jest?'

'No, Princess. No breeches this morning — step into this, if you please.'

Arrosa was on her knees in front of me, holding the kirtle. I stepped in, hauled the waistband up and tied the strings. Karmele placed the shirt over my shoulders and my arms into the sleeves, and Alazne tied it up and fiddled with a sheer mantilla and the coronet to cover my hair.

'Thank you,' I murmured as they stepped back to have a look. They were all wearing black.

'Javier has emptied a wagon for us to travel together, so we can arrive with dignity,' said Arrosa.

I looked at her carefully. She and Javier seemed to be near each other quite often, and her face lit up at the mention of his name.

'Let us leave, Princess,' said Karmele, and they handed me down the steps of the wagon.

Captain Javier's jaw dropped when he spotted me coming towards him. 'Princess Berengaria, you are a vision.' He was standing by a new horse and dropped onto one knee, which I stepped on.

'What's this for?' I demanded, looking at a knob on the front of the saddle.

'It's a horn,' said Javier.

'Cock your leg over it,' advised Arrosa.

I spun and threw a leg over the horn so as to sit on the horse with both legs on one side.

'This is strange,' I said. 'Won't I fall off?'

'Keep a tight grip of it with your thighs,' said Arrosa, saving Javier from further explanation.

Alazne was by this time of no use, being consumed with mirth. I did as instructed and felt more secure.

'How do I guide the beast?' I demanded. 'I cannot use both feet.'

'The reins, Your Highness,' said Javier. 'Use only the reins.'

I tried it out and pulled back on the reins, bringing the horse to a halt while I waited for Javier to catch up. He was not alone; two columns of his men rode by, one each side of me. I was destined to arrive at the church of Blessed Mary in style, and I hoped that Eleanor would witness it.

My mood brightened when we approached the church. There was a crowd waiting, and they began to cheer as I approached. Eleanor was in conversation with some important-looking people outside, so she heard the people welcoming me.

I was now well in control of my steed and brought her to a halt as close to Eleanor as I could. Then two of Javier's riders appeared at my side, and they kneeled on one knee each so that I could dismount. It was perfect. I stood still as Alazne shook out my kirtle and Arrosa appeared at my side to complete the tidying of my attire.

Then Eleanor noticed me. A range of expressions crossed her wrinkled face, and she evidently decided to make the best of it as she beckoned me forward.

'This is my son's betrothed, Bishop Ranier,' she said curtly, as if she couldn't remember my name.

The bishop, a tall man of some distinction, offered me a hand. His eyes twinkled as he welcomed me. 'Princess Berengaria, welcome. We have heard much about you, and I see that reports of your beauty have not been exaggerated. You will grace our church, I'm sure.'

'Thank you, Bishop Ranier. You are most kind. These are my ladies.' I gestured behind me, where Alazne and Arrosa were standing like black statues.

'Ladies.' He nodded in their direction, receiving sparkling smiles and curtsies in return. He then turned to Eleanor. 'If you would enter, Queen Eleanor, the verger will direct you inside. I will be off to prepare to lead the service.'

So saying, he moved to the church door, crozier in hand, and disappeared inside. I was left facing Eleanor, uncertain of her reaction, but she surprised me.

After looking me up and down, she smiled. 'The bishop is observant. You are beautiful. I only hope that Richard can take his eyes off his duties for long enough to appreciate what he has been blessed with. Come, Berengaria, take my arm and we will enter together.'

Karmele arrived, having been brought by wagon, and my entourage was complete.

Eleanor and I did not speak further until after the service. When we gathered outside afterwards, she exchanged a few warm words with the bishop and accepted his invitation to his buffet, a pre-Christmas celebration.

Nearby was a grand marquee by the sea, with braziers and fires burning outside to spit-roast hunks of meat. Inside, buffet tables were set out. Some way off I noticed that tables had been provided outside for the ordinary folk, with plenty of wine and food.

The business of meeting so many people who wanted to congratulate me or engage in tittle-tattle made the afternoon very tedious. With relief I watched Eleanor being escorted back to her caravan, and my ladies and I soon made our escape, leaving behind an increasingly noisy crowd of revellers.

Our little caravan was camped in a quiet spot, tightly gathered and carefully guarded so that it was easy to escape the crowd. 'We are bound for Italy in the morning,' I reminded my ladies. 'Pass that wine flagon, and liven up that fire, Alazne.'

We rose early, for Eleanor was worried that we would not be able to traverse the Alpes Maritimes if we dawdled.

'How far is it?' Arrosa asked Captain Javier.

I had noticed that the two of them had been exchanging glances more and more regularly.

'About two hundred and forty miles along the Via Aurelia, my lady,' he replied.

'Call me by my name, if you wish, Captain,' said Arrosa.

Javier smiled. He was handsome, and I thought they might look well together, given some encouragement. He looked across at me for permission.

I smiled and nodded.

'Then call me Javier ... Arrosa,' he said.

Alazne and I mounted our horses, and then she leaned across. 'Those two?' she whispered.

I urged my horse forward. 'Let's watch them; it helps to pass the time.'

We soon left the sea behind as we wound our way upwards. The track bent back and forth, with villages becoming further apart the higher we climbed. Though it was cold at night, the days were tolerable and I often dismounted to walk alongside my horse. It eased the stiffness in my legs and gave the horse a rest.

We celebrated Christmas Day during the journey. Father Petri took the opportunity to remind us that Christ had suffered for our sins, so we should be grateful that we would soon be back down from the hills.

The morning after the day after Christmas, I was woken by Alazne stirring in her berth.

'Morning, my princess!' she called.

'Morning, ladies,' I replied.

Alazne reached over to pull back Arrosa's curtain. There was no one in her bed. 'Where is she? It is full light.'

At that moment, Arrosa came up the steps and entered. Seeing us peering at her, she blushed. 'I … I've been out watering the plants.'

'Really?' I said. 'You tidied your bed before you left, I see. It hardly seems slept in. Have you seen Captain Javier on your watering mission?'

'I've heard that he has a tent somewhere, a little distant from his men,' observed Alazne.

Arrosa avoided answering. 'I'll help you to dress, Princess. There's food out here; we will be leaving soon.'

After four days of climbing and three days descending, we came in sight of the sea at Fréjus. We then spent a day travelling to Canua, where Eleanor occupied the château at Le Suquet for one night.

After we had left there, I sought out Karmele during one of our stops. 'Have you noticed the affection between Arrosa and Javier?' I asked her.

'Yes, they are well fitted and good souls,' she replied. 'The problem is, can you do without them?'

'Why cannot they continue to serve me, Karmele?'

'I believe that if they are given any encouragement, Arrosa will be with child by the end of the week.'

'So I shouldn't take her to the Holy Land?'

'I am not sure, Princess.' Karmele drew in a deep breath. 'And now I must speak about Alazne. She cares too much for you, and you allow her too much freedom.'

'Really? But she is my personal servant — how can she be too close?'

'Believe me, Princess, there are women who prefer other women; it is written in history.'

I did not find Karmele's worries that surprising. 'Has Alazne said anything?'

'No, but I have watched her. She blossoms when you are near and fades when you are not. I may be wrong, but be careful. You are about to get married.'

'Yes, something like that might alter Eleanor's view of me. Thank you, Karmele, I'll think carefully about the things you have shared with me. Now, let's get back. Eleanor will be miles ahead by now.'

As we neared the camp, I could see Captain Javier on the beach, talking with his sergeants. As we approached, he dismissed them and stood looking out towards the Lérins Islands. He then turned to greet me. 'Hello, Your Highness.'

'You were briefing your sergeants for the day, Captain?'

'Yes, Your Highness. I need to remind them about standards. They had become slack in dress and familiarity…'

'I agree — the very subject that Maîtresse Karmele and I have been talking about. This caravan is the court of Navarre *en route*, and we are in the company of the court of Aquitaine, if not that of England. Standards are important, and we should maintain them.'

'I agree,' he replied, shuffling his feet.

'Arrosa should be in her proper place at all times, do you not agree?'

'I do, Your Highness. I'm sorry.' He looked crestfallen.

'Arrosa is young and has been within the confines of the palace all her life. She may be unworldly in some matters; do not take advantage of her.'

'It is not my intention, Your Highness. I had something else in mind.'

'Something permanent? Are you asking for permission to marry my tending lady?'

'I … things have come along since we left Olite. We had been talking before we left.'

'Had you? Well, until things change, ensure that these talks do not occupy her at night; she sleeps with us.'

'Sorry, Your Highness.' He stood looking at the sea until I released him from his torture.

'I will speak with Arrosa. Until then, daytime only.'

He brightened up considerably and gave me a little bow. 'You would bless a marriage, Your Highness?'

'If Arrosa is agreeable, yes, Captain Javier, I would.'

CHAPTER FIVE

For the next part of the journey we clung to narrow tracks between mountains and water, at times in danger of falling into the Ligurian Sea. When we came to transition from France into Liguria, Javier explained to me the importance of the region within the network of Italian city states, of which I knew little. I now understood that la Repubblica di Genova was one of them, and self-governing within the Holy Roman Empire.

Eventually we reached the port of Genova. During this difficult part of our travels, I had not managed to go forward to speak with Eleanor, but as soon as the road permitted I guided my horse forward to see what she had to say.

When we came up to Eleanor's caravan, they were all arranged in an open area near the harbour, the great walls of the city towering above us. We formed our camp behind the queen's contingent, and together with Captain Javier and an escort of six I rode forward between the formidable city walls and the quayside towards a great open area near a city gate. As we approached, I could see that Eleanor was out of her wagon and surrounded by quite a crowd. We had arrived at about midday, and evidently the visit of the Queen of England had caused some excitement.

'Ah!' she said so all could hear. 'The princess has decided to grace us with her presence.'

I dismounted and walked over. There was a churchman beside Eleanor.

'Monsignor Parelli, allow me to introduce Princess Berengaria of Navarre, soon to be married to my son Richard, King of England.'

I bowed and murmured, 'If our paths ever cross, *monsignor.*'

Eleanor gave one of her mirthless laughs. 'The princess has a wicked sense of humour. Monsignor Parelli is dean to Archbishop Boniface. He has news of Richard and an invitation to attend the archbishop in his palace near San Lorenzo's cathedral. We should be properly dressed to accept this invitation, if you could manage one of your gowns, my dear?'

'*Si, Principessa* Berengaria, the archbishop is very particular on such things,' said Monsignor Parelli.

'Worry not, *monsignor.* I am amply supplied with gowns. But what of King Richard? We see many ships in the harbour.'

'Ah, the redoubtable warrior, your betrothed. He visited here to enquire after the health of King Philip of France. The French king does not travel well by sea, it seems, and he rested here for a few days. But both kings have left. Despite his doubts, Philip intends to sail directly to Outremer, and Richard is sailing down the coast to Naples. I understand that they argued about some matters.'

'Really?' Queen Eleanor perked up at the mention of an argument. She was perhaps wondering if Richard had finally revealed his repudiation of the French princess, Alys, to her brother. 'And what dispute was that, *monsignor?*'

'Oh, something about ships. Philip seemed to resent the numbers that Richard has at his disposal; they are coming from all over to go and join him at Akko. They are stuffed with men, horses, and other supplies.'

Eleanor smiled. 'Then Philip ought to have prepared properly for this venture, as I'm sure my son has. When are we expected at the archbishop's palace, Monsignor Parelli?'

'When the sun goes down, *altezza.* I will come with suitable coaches and conduct you directly.' He cast an eye in my direction before he issued what I took as a command, although it was given gently enough. 'There will be no need to be riding a horse, as there will be two coaches for our royal guests.'

I returned to our small encampment. There was much excitement when I informed Alazne and Arrosa of the event planned for the evening, and they became engaged in a heated discussion regarding my dress. Karmele didn't seem keen to go, so I gave her permission to remain. The other two settled on a green gown for me.

I went to rest in my wagon. I was not looking forward to an evening with the archbishop, who, I had been informed, was also the temporal ruler in Genova. I had hardly closed my eyes when the curtain was thrown back and two beaming faces peered in at me.

'We're ready, Princess,' said Arrosa, displaying the finery chosen for me.

'Out of those things,' ordered Alazne, tugging at my boots.

Soon I was being slipped into a grand gown. I looked demure yet sparkling — fit to visit the ruler of Genova.

I inspected the clothes that the pair had chosen for themselves. 'You two look splendid, and I shall be very proud of you. Has that coach arrived yet?'

Arrosa poked her head out of the back of the wagon. 'Yes. Captain Javier is here, and there is a coach surrounded by lots of lovely men.'

I looked out. There were many men in what I supposed were the uniforms of the Archbishop of Genova. Monsignor Parelli was not waiting there. I supposed that he had gone to collect Queen Eleanor, but some other priestly officer was waiting for us.

'*Principessa*,' he called brightly, 'I am Umberto, Monsignor Parelli's secretary. He is with the queen and sends his apologies. If you would allow my humble self to accompany you, we will go straight to the palace of Archbishop Boniface.'

'My pleasure, *padre*. May I call you *padre*?'

'*Si, Principessa*, Padre Umberto suits me well.'

He held out a hand and I climbed into the coach, which rocked from side to side. This did not improve when Arrosa and Alazne squeezed in and Padre Umberto settled next to Alazne. Then we set off along the quayside, accompanied by a cheering crowd all the way up to what Umberto told us was the Via Lorenzo. We stopped outside a grand building. Umberto left first to prepare the way, and after a moment we followed. There were wide steps up to the entrance, lined with soldiers. Two on each side at the top had trumpets, which they blew into with gusto as we climbed.

'Welcome to the palace of His Grace the Archbishop of Genova,' proclaimed Monsignor Parelli, backed up by his secretary, Umberto, who was smiling at Alazne unctuously.

Alazne snorted and both women stuck close to me as we progressed along a sumptuously lined corridor. Statues, paintings, tapestries, busts and specimens of exquisite glassware all betokened extreme wealth and privilege. Alazne and Arrosa fell silent as we arrived before a very tall door.

Monsignor Parelli spoke to me gently. 'With your permission, *Principessa* Berengaria, we will take your ladies to another room, where they will be fed in the company of some of the fine ladies of Genova. The queen's ladies are already in there, so they are in good company. Padre Umberto will escort them.'

I nodded my approval — I could hardly refuse. Alazne pulled a face but Arrosa scuttled after Umberto, anxious to see this collection of fine ladies, no doubt.

The doors swung open to reveal a small dining chamber. The walls were lined with bookshelves, and the centre was occupied by a splendid wooden table. The man I presumed was Boniface sat at one end, and on his right was Eleanor. Monsignor Parelli seated me opposite Eleanor, and she gave me one of her best smiles.

The archbishop did not rise as I sat, but he seemed a pleasant enough man, and he addressed me gently. '*Principessa*, the tales of your beauty have lacked some detail; they have not been fulsome enough. Queen Eleanor, I see that your son is to be a very fortunate man.'

'Indeed, Archbishop. She is pious and beautiful, a rare combination.'

'Then we shall have a splendid evening. Monsignor Parelli will sit behind me, to assist both my languages and my memory. When we have had a little to eat, we will discuss matters of importance. You agree, Queen Eleanor?'

'I do, Your Eminence. While my son is scudding across the waves to rescue Jerusalem, there are matters of state to be dealt with here.'

'Indeed, indeed.'

Although the archbishop was surrounded by servants offering food and drink, the archbishop refused much, being content with a few delicacies and a little of the well-decanted wines. I followed suit, as I thought I might need to be in full control of my wits tonight.

Archbishop Boniface, evidently not a man to waste time on trivialities, soon had the table cleared, apart from a silver decanter, which he indicated. 'To make you feel at home, *Principessa*, a fine wine from your homeland.'

Indeed it was: a full and fruity dark red Basque wine.

'Ah, Rioja Alavesa? I compliment you on your choice, Your Eminence; the taste is very recognisable.'

'Thank you, *Principessa*. Did you enjoy the delicacies of my table?'

'We did, Your Eminence,' said Eleanor. 'The road is long and tedious at times.'

'But the cause is just. Removing the unholy from the Holy City will make all the sacrifices worthwhile, I'm certain.'

'My son will do his best, I'm sure.'

'Ah, indeed,' replied the archbishop, 'which brings us to a question. Last June, as you may know, Barbarossa fell off his horse into a river in Anatolia, and drowned.'

'The Holy Roman Emperor,' said Eleanor imperiously, looking at me as if I did not know who Frederick Barbarossa was.

'Yes,' continued Boniface with a sigh, 'and now his successor, Heinrich the Sixth, King of Germany, is on his way to Rome to be installed as the new Holy Roman Emperor.'

'Yes, and that is good?' asked Eleanor.

'It may be, *altezza*, but it leaves your son, and the French king, Philip, with a problem. When Frederick left this earth, his army, which he was leading to join the Crusade, took Frederick's death as an omen, and most of the soldiers decided to leave Anatolia and flee back to Germany.'

'How many?' asked Eleanor, shocked.

'Oh, some say one hundred thousand, others say ten thousand. Your son and, no doubt, King Philip were expecting a lot of help from them which is no longer there.'

'Is my betrothed aware of this?' I asked.

'Probably, but he sailed past the mouth of the Tiber. Pope Innocent was expecting him to call so that they might discuss the problem.'

'Where is he now?' I asked.

'He called at Pisa and Napoli and may now be in Sicily.'

'My daughter, Joan,' cried Eleanor, losing her composure for a moment. 'He has gone to rescue her from that beast, Tancred.'

'No doubt, but he may have left a ship for you ladies in the river Arno near Pisa, or perhaps at Napoli.'

'So, Your Eminence, how does all this affect us?' I asked. 'Have we any part to play in this great game?'

'Heinrich is on his way to Rome. His Holiness the Pope wishes you to go and meet Heinrich before he reaches there and have a little talk with him. The purpose is twofold. First, we want to know if Heinrich intends to replace the troops who have gone missing in Anatolia. Richard and Philip must have reinforcements if they are to succeed.'

'And second?' asked Eleanor.

'It concerns your daughter, Joan.'

'Indeed. Now that her husband King William of Sicily is deceased, she is by right Queen of Sicily. But her position is not guaranteed if Heinrich has his way,' said Eleanor, glowering.

'Indeed,' said Boniface, 'the question of succession is in the air.'

'I'm lost,' I confessed. 'Which part of the story have I missed?'

Boniface looked at Eleanor for permission to explain, which she gave with a nod.

'Joan may be queen, but she and King William had no issue. However, her husband William had a cousin, named Tancred, who thinks that it entitles him to a tilt at the crown of Sicily. He is the issue of Roger, Duke of Apulia and a mistress named Emma. Tancred, being both an unpleasant person and a bastard, is not the perfect choice as King of Sicily and half of Italy. You might agree, *Principessa*?'

'I have not considered the problem very much. So who is?'

'A Siciliana. Constance, the daughter of King Roger the second of Sicily.' Seeing my blank expression, Boniface explained further. 'Joan's husband, William, pronounced Constance heir presumptive in 1172 after her nephew Henry of Capua — the next natural heir — died, and when he and Joan did not produce a direct heir.'

'She became Queen Regnant, and married the soon-to-be-emperor, King Heinrich,' Eleanor added. 'She was born after her father died; he never got to see her.'

'Does she take precedence over Joan?' I asked.

'Empress Constance, in the eyes of political expediency, may be recognised as the next Queen of Sicily.'

'What does Joan make of this?'

'We do not know for certain because Tancred has her locked up. But the declaration by her husband William that Constance would be Queen Regnant in the event that they did not produce issue was supported by Joan. She may not have wanted the position for herself if William died first.' Boniface paused. 'I will tell you both of His Holiness's wish. When you speak to Heinrich seek more troops from Germany for your son, Queen Eleanor, and tell him that the way is clear for Constance to take up her duties as Queen of Sicily and Italy whenever that can be arranged. Ensure that he understands that the two issues are in some way connected, and one would expedite the achievement of the other.'

I could see Eleanor's jaw working. Finally, she spoke. 'This will be the end of Norman rule in the south. The Hautevilles fought off many enemies for control of Sicily and southern Italy. Robert Guiscard, Bohemund the great warrior and

Robert of Normandy — himself the saviour of Jerusalem and uncle to my husband — all their efforts will be wasted.'

'They will not be forgotten, dear lady. Their history is written, but times move on, and there are new problems and new solutions. His Holiness is minded to move on from the previous animosity of Mother Church to the Hohenstaufen dynasty. Besides, we need the Germans to support our Crusade — is that not what Richard would want?'

After a struggle, Eleanor rallied. 'The Crusade must have precedence, of course. My son must have all the soldiers possible for this holy cause. You have set out matters most admirably, Your Eminence. I must write to Richard; he must be given hope, and I need to know that poor Joan is safe and well.'

'Of course, *altezza*. We can help in that regard. I have fast galleys in the harbour, and I will place one at your disposal. You may write to Richard wherever he may be, from wherever you may be, and it will be taken to him. A small reward for your understanding in this most important matter of state, and for Mother Church.'

'Thank you, Your Eminence. But it has been a long day...'

'Of course, we must not keep you. I have enjoyed this evening in most charming and helpful company. It is a rare thing for a man such as myself, and I may find the time to do it again.'

I awoke early the next morning. Alazne was still asleep, Arrosa was stirring and Karmele was already up.

I dressed and went to sit on the wagon steps as Javier turned up.

'Morning, Princess. There is a clear sky — it should be nice later.'

'Yes. Arrosa will be out soon,' I said.

'You went to see the archbishop last night? I believe that he wields all the power in this city.'

I looked at him in the strengthening light. I trusted him, and I needed to speak to someone. 'Javier, I was once happy helping my father to rule Navarre. I understood what was required and I felt able to be useful. But I have realised how small Navarre is. Now, we have been cast into a game that stretches across Europe and into Outremer, across the sea. I feel quite small.'

'What has transpired, Princess?'

'We are to meet with the Emperor Elect, Heinrich, to ask him to provide more troops for the Crusade, and remind him that he is going to Rome to be installed as emperor by Pope Innocent … but only if he is compliant in certain matters.'

'That sounds like a bargain of sorts. If it was taken the wrong way, he might not comply.'

'Eleanor is to remind him that papal support is needed for his wife, Constance, to take up her duties as Queen of Sicily, and that it is still in abeyance.'

'I thought that Joan was left as Queen of Sicily when William died?'

'As Eleanor's daughter, she can find a more comfortable position elsewhere, I'm sure.'

'Indeed, but now I see the size of the game that we are in,' Javier replied. 'The queen has a message for you, Princess. If you want to send a note to Richard, present it at her galley by mid-morning.'

'I'll find my writing things. Will these notes be safe, Javier? I do not want prying eyes to see my messages.'

'I believe that the queen is sending her personal courier on board to carry her writings safely to their destination. I'll be away now, Princess.' He hesitated and fiddled with his hands.

I knew what he wished to hear. 'You are wondering whether I have spoken with Arrosa. I'll do it now. Off you go.'

Javier left with a smile, whistling a cheerful tune.

I called for Arrosa and motioned for her to sit next to me on the steps. 'Arrosa, you are sixteen, I think?'

'Last birthday, Princess.'

'You are in love with that bearded oaf?'

'Your Highness!' she gasped, standing up.

'Sit down. I jest — I couldn't imagine a better choice for a husband. I trust that you will both be gloriously happy forever.'

Her jaw dropped. With a squeal, she threw herself into my arms and then set off after Javier.

I went back into the wagon to find that Alazne had risen. 'Find my writing implements, please, Alazne. I seem to have lost Arrosa.'

CHAPTER SIX

It was midday by the time we set off. As we left the harbour area, I spied a fast galley cleaving through the water — my letter was on its way, and whatever Eleanor had despatched.

We were heading for Milano this time, another hundred miles or so. I would have two or three nights to consider the web of intrigue that stretched across continents. Not even the redoubtable Eleanor was anything more than a pawn in the great game.

By the end of January, we had turned inland and left the milder sea air behind us, so the evenings soon turned chilly. One night, Javier brought a summons from Eleanor, and I went to see what she wanted.

When I reached Eleanor's encampment, I was escorted to her night wagon, which was different from her day wagon. It was a little longer, seen from the outside, and as I entered I saw that the back of it was a little office, with benches along the sides and a table fixed in the centre.

'You sent for me, Your Highness?'

'Sit opposite me, if you will, Berengaria. I want a little talk.' She gestured at a man sitting at the head of the table, surrounded by papers, pens and inks, with a candle on each side of him. He looked up and smiled.

'You'll remember Father Herbert, my clerk. Do not mind him; he only listens when I tell him to.' She smiled at him, and he returned to his scribbling. 'I wanted to ask if you've had any thoughts on the meeting with Boniface.'

'I have,' I responded. 'It seems that you and I are to be ambassadors and negotiators to the Papal See. Am I right, Your Highness?'

She gazed at me. 'Unfortunately, that is also what I had discerned. We are to barter my daughter for troops for my son, and give away a kingdom into the bargain.'

'He is a clever diplomat, the archbishop. He made it all seem reasonable and logical, as if there was no other resolution possible.'

'That's what bothers me most; I should have seen it coming. I must be slipping into my dotage.'

I chuckled. 'Not from what I have seen, Your Highness.'

'Well, as far as I can see, I will have to go through with it. My late husband Henry slipped in and out of excommunication while he lived, and I have no intention of following that pattern. I'll do what Pope Innocent is expecting of me and try to be more perspicacious in future.' Then she issued an invitation. 'Sit with me awhile, my dear. I miss the company of others at times. I'm stuck with that scribbler every night, and I go to bed early when I have done the day's business. Isn't that the case, Father Herbert?'

'Indeed, Your Highness. You work too much.'

'Indeed I do. Wine!' she called, and one of her ladies appeared with a carafe and two glasses. She turned to me. 'I noted that you drank sparingly when we met with the archbishop. Do you not imbibe?'

'Not when I need my wits about me, and that night was one such.'

'Wisdom, in one so beautiful, is a rare event. Now, let us discuss weddings and suchlike.'

A little while later, I had time to reflect as I travelled the short distance from Eleanor's wagon back to mine. I had gathered several things during our conversation. Richard was a saint, but John, whom they had left in charge in England, was a worry; the Pope was devious, and the reason we were not travelling by sea was because Eleanor suffered from seasickness.

After riding through the rain for much of the following morning, we had begun to steam in a weak afternoon sun when the caravan came to an abrupt halt.

'Send someone forward and find out why we have stopped, Captain Javier,' I said as he pulled alongside me.

'I'll go myself; it might be something important.' He issued orders to his sergeants. 'Take up defensive positions: there are reports of bandits in this area. I'm going forward to speak to the queen's guard.' He galloped off.

It was not long before he was back.

'The queen has received an emissary, Princess, a Benedictine courier. There has been a meeting arranged for her with the German king, Heinrich, at the Palazzo Vescovile in the town of Lodi.'

'He is not Emperor yet?'

'Seems not. We are not going to Milano; we will change direction. Lodi is further south, another day's ride.'

The next evening saw us approach the town of Lodi, a settlement that predated Roman times. It had an important bridge over the river Adda and, being a place of narrow streets, I was told that it was all laid out in straight lines. The area was filled with soldiers in strange garb.

'Germans,' said Javier and ordered everyone to stay closer together. We were kept outside the town itself. Eleanor's officials argued at length, but in the end the only compromise was to allow her two-wheeled chariot to enter. I would remain mounted, which was no bother to them, but if King Heinrich expected to see me in a court gown he would be disappointed. Javier arranged for our encampment to be enjoined with Eleanor's, to keep us as safe as possible.

After word had been sent into the town, some important-looking Germans were allowed into Eleanor's encampment, and soon I was summoned to go and join her. I was asked to leave my ladies behind, but I could take an escort of six with Javier at the head. I also took Father Petri — we couldn't deprive him of a visit to an archbishop's palace, and I was sure that Father Herbert would be stuck to Eleanor's side.

Forming up behind Eleanor's chariot, we followed when she and her escort set off.

There weren't many locals nearby. The place swarmed with Germans, lounging and swapping rude remarks as I rode past. I had some knowledge of the language, and their tone was clear.

It was a relief to arrive at the *palazzo*, although we were not led directly to its entrance. Instead, we were led into the walled garden that fronted the main building. Here Javier was instructed to wait with my guard while I was escorted inside.

Eleanor was waiting in the garden with two of her ladies, properly begowned. Her face showed some relief when I appeared; it was clear that she was not comfortable with the situation.

'Well, Berengaria, we appear to have arrived at a German festival.'

'I did notice. We couldn't get here any sooner because of the crowds. Let's go in,' I said impulsively. 'We might stir up some interest.'

'You are a bold one. Ah! Here is someone, at last.'

An official was hurrying towards us: a churchman in flying skirts and skullcap.

'Your Highness, Your Highness, forgive me. I had not expected you so early, and I have only just finished escorting the emperor. I am *Legato* Benedetto, papal emissary to the Holy Roman Emperor, Heinrich.'

'He is not emperor yet,' Eleanor muttered to me. She then turned her best smile upon the puffing cardinal. 'Not to worry, Your Eminence. You are here now. Pray tell me, what is intended next?'

'We will go to a private chamber to discuss matters of importance with His Holiness.'

'Very well. But before we go, you might like to be introduced to the future Queen of England, the betrothed of my son King Richard, Princess Berengaria.'

That was unexpected but welcome. Prior to that I had been half hidden behind Eleanor and ignored by the cardinal, but now she stepped back. I watched Benedetto's eyebrows rise and his jaw drop as he took in my road-besmirched riding attire.

'*Principessa* Berengaria, how rude of me.' He managed to recover admirably, as a good diplomat should. 'We have heard so much about you. It is a great pleasure to meet you.'

He held out a hand and I remembered the ring. I touched his hand lightly and brushed my lips across this symbol of heavenly power on earth.

He spoke again. 'Dear child of God, so much is expected of you. I pray that God will guide you and give you strength. *In nomine Patris et Filii et Spiritus Sancti.*'

'*Amen*,' Eleanor and I responded.

'I see your priests, *altezza*?'

'Mine,' Eleanor and I chorused, smiling. I waited for her to beckon Father Herbert, then I signalled Father Petri forward for his chance to kiss the cardinal's ring. He faded into the background immediately after that, while we were escorted into an anteroom in the palace with drinks and small plates of food.

'What do you want us to do, Your Eminence?' asked Eleanor.

'The situation is like this, *altezza*. We have word that Heinrich does not like the idea of negotiating with a woman...'

'Me?' Eleanor bridled. 'I am Queen of England. I speak for the king.'

'That too disturbs the emperor; he is no great admirer of Richard.'

'So how can we move forward, Your Eminence?' I asked.

'There is a way. We have Heinrich sitting quietly in another chamber with his advisors. If you remain here, I will carry the discussion hither and thither until there is an agreement. Then you can meet and confirm the agreement in a charter, if that is acceptable, *altezza*?'

Eleanor looked at me; at this moment, she need an ally. Taking me by the hand, she addressed the cardinal. 'If you would give us a moment, *Legato* Benedetto?'

'Of course.' He moved to the far side of the room.

'We have discussed this at length, Your Highness,' I said. 'My views have not altered. Heinrich shall have Sicily — if His Holiness is satisfied with him as Emperor of the Holy Roman Empire, and then only if he provides King Richard with German soldiers for the Crusade.'

Eleanor looked at Benedetto. 'You heard that, Your Eminence?'

He nodded. 'I did, and this is our desired outcome. But I may need to persuade Heinrich along the path to righteousness.' He grinned conspiratorially. 'This should not be the opening offer. Heinrich must find his way towards it.'

'Then we may be here some time, Your Eminence?' asked Eleanor.

'Not at all, *altezza*. Heinrich is expected in Rome before long, and the Pope is a busy man.'

He left, humming a tune, but soon returned. Eleanor and I looked at each other; it couldn't have been that easy, surely.

'*Altezza, Principessa,* we are close to an agreement. The emperor wants something of little concern to England or Navarre.'

'Which is?' asked Eleanor suspiciously.

'It is the case that the prince-bishops in this region guard the pilgrim's way from over the Alps down to Rome. They are known as *Fürstbischof* in German. The present incumbent is Conrad the second of Biseno. He was appointed by Emperor Barbarossa, and Heinrich would like his position to be confirmed.'

'What do they do, these *Fürstbischof?*' I enquired of him.

'They issue coin and collect tolls. A perfect circle, you see,' Benedetto said with a twinkle in his eye.

'Some of these tolls might find their way into the papal coffers, no doubt,' said Eleanor.

'Crusades are expensive, of that there is no doubt. I can agree to this, and, as a gesture of good faith, I can ask you, *altezza*, if you would sign a charter confirming Conrad in his appointment?'

'We will be co-signatories?'

'Indeed, and as one with the Church. A most satisfactory outcome, do you not think?' Despite his apparent confidence, Benedetto didn't meet our eyes. I decided to draw him out.

'There are a lot of Heinrich's soldiers around,' I observed. 'He is fully supported...?'

'Ah, yes, *Principessa*, very observant. Queen Eleanor, do you happen to have a crown in your baggage?'

'I do. Has King Heinrich set up a court in there?' she asked, nodding towards the door.

'He wants to command the chamber a little,' Benedetto replied.

'How much time do we have, Your Eminence?'

'A little. I can stall while the clerics finish writing the charter.'

'Adelaide,' Eleanor spoke to one of her ladies, 'go outside and ask one of my escort to take you back to the encampment, you know where to find my crown, and sort something suitable for our princess.'

'Yes, highness.' And she dashed out of the chamber.

'Tell me more about Heinrich, Your Eminence, and how best to deal with him.'

'Come with me, *altezza*.'

He led Eleanor to the far end of the chamber. Standing in front of the ornate fireplace, they engaged in some intimate and enlivened conversation.

I took the opportunity to bring Father Petri out of his overawed trance. 'Have you ever married anyone outside a church, Father?'

'Oh, yes, in the summer, in olive and orange groves, Princess.'

'Well, would you like to marry Arrosa and Javier?'

'Really? Upon my soul, have I missed something? I'm usually quite observant. My, my, I'd like that. I'll find my chalice. Ah, here are your clothes.'

Eleanor's interview had lasted quite a while, and they had barely finished when Adelaide came puffing back into the chamber, followed by bundle-carrying servants.

As Eleanor was already in a gown, she only needed a fine caul and her crown upon her head to complete her ensemble. With me, it would be a little more difficult.

Legato Benedetto looked me up and down and sighed. My black hair ran wild, and I wore a padded gambeson over a plain white shirt. My lower half was clad in a pair of close-cut breeches and kid leather riding boots.

Eleanor looked at Adelaide. 'Have you brought aught else?'

Adelaide, grinning, shook out another bundle. In it was a long black cloak with a fur-lined hood. When it unfurled, a loop of pearls fell from its folds.

'Yes, that'll do. Quickly now, I see that the cardinal grows impatient.'

I was soon enveloped in the cloak. Adelaide had the pearls twisted into my hair, which she topped with another gauze caul. She stood back, proud of her work.

Eleanor clapped her hands and turned to Benedetto. 'Will that be suitable, Your Eminence?'

'Very,' he smiled. 'Keep the cloak closed, and try to keep the boots beneath the folds. Now we go.'

The cardinal escorted us to a larger chamber, where we found Heinrich already in place.

Sitting on one side of a great table, surrounded by his court and backed by a row of soldiers — with no weapons, I noticed — was a middle-aged man with flowing blond locks. He occupied one large chair and was flanked by his advisors. He was polite enough to stand when Queen Eleanor entered the chamber.

Benedetto escorted Eleanor to an equally large chair opposite Heinrich, and I was placed on her left while Benedetto sat himself down on her right. At each end of the table sat a scribe — one for the German and one for the cardinal. This conversation was to be recorded in case of any future controversy. I looked behind me, pleased to see that Father Petri had followed us in; he would remember what transpired.

'Queen Eleanor, I am happy to meet you,' said Heinrich.

'King Heinrich, we too are happy to meet you. May I introduce Princess Berengaria, the betrothed of my son Richard?'

Heinrich stood once more and bowed in my direction. 'Then your son is truly blessed, Eleanor. I greet you warmly, *Prinzessin* Berengaria. Are you cold?' he asked, observing my tightly held cloak. 'I'll have them build up the fire.' He indicated the fireplace at the end of the chamber.

'Please don't trouble yourself, Your Highness. I'm comfortable as I am. I wish not to interrupt the proceedings.'

'Indeed, indeed. Eleanor, I believe that we have an agreement?'

'We have, Heinrich. It only remains to sign it.'

'Good, and when do you expect to find the redoubtable Richard?' he said, glancing at me again.

'We will off to Pisa in the morning. There should be news from there, God willing.'

'*Wie Gott es will.* There are two charters to sign, are there not?'

Benedetto waved at his clerk and the parchments appeared before us. Heinrich signed first and passed the vellums across the table for Eleanor, who signed and gave them to Benedetto. He too signed and placed the papal seal on them. Then they went down the table to Heinrich's clerk, who placed the

German seal upon them with a flourish. This exercise was repeated twice more, until everyone had a copy.

'Good, good. Is that complete now, *Legato* Benedetto?'

'Indeed it is, and these may well be the last papers you will sign as King Heinrich. Soon you will be, by the grace of God, Holy Roman Emperor.'

With our business completed, we said our farewells. When we emerged from the palace, the cold night air penetrated my cloak and shirt.

'Where's my gambeson?' I asked.

Alazne, who had been standing in the chilly garden, came forth and handed it over.

'What did you and the cardinal talk about when you were by the fireplace, Your Highness?' I asked Eleanor as her ladies got her ready for the short journey back.

'Ah, this you should be aware of. The emperor's family, the Hohenstaufens, want the position of emperor to be made hereditary. The Pope does not agree. It places too much power in their hands, which would not be wrested from them easily, but...'

'But he wants them to provide troops.'

'Indeed, so the Pope is moving very slowly on the matter, with vague promises and so forth.'

'But what if the troops also turn out to be ... vague?'

'Yes, that is a concern. We'll have to wait and see how it develops. Perhaps there will be more certainty when Heinrich meets Pope Innocent. Come on, let's get back. We will be on the road towards Pisa in the morning. I trust that Richard has left a ship there for us; I tire of that damned rattling wagon. Would you ride closer to me tomorrow? We really must share some things.'

'Of course,' I replied, trying to keep the astonishment out of my voice.

'Are you ready, Princess?' Captain Javier called into the back of my wagon the following day.

'One moment,' I replied, shrugging into my gambeson. 'How far this time, Javier?' I asked as I stepped down from the wagon.

'About one hundred and sixty miles, Princess.'

'Is the road by the sea?'

'It will cross the *Monti Appennini*, Princess, before we can travel along the Ligurian coast once more.'

'I pray that Richard has left us a ship. What is Pisa like, Javier?'

'It is one of the Italian city states, near the end of the river Arno. It has a big harbour, with many ships. The city trades throughout the world, rivalling Genova and Venetia in sea power. That's what I know, Princess.'

'And it is nearly two weeks away?'

'If the mountain passes remain free of snow. Shall we leave now, Princess?'

'Yes, I must not let the queen leave before me. But first, I have arranged for you and Arrosa to be wed. I'm afraid you will need to wait a while longer until some convenient stop.'

He stared at me, lost for words.

'I'd better leave,' I said. 'Karmele, Arrosa and Alazne will be safe following along with the rest of your men, Javier?'

'Oh, yes, thank you, Princess. We will take only four of mine and yet be secure within Eleanor's caravan — God knows there are enough of them.' He grinned and started to hum.

With everything arranged, I climbed onto my horse with the help of a soldier's knee, and then set off to join Eleanor.

After two days of riding south with the *Appennini* on our right, we turned towards them at Fontanellato, near Parma. The next part of the journey would be through those mountains.

I returned to my sleeping wagon to wash and eat every evening. Lacking facilities in the mountains, I resorted to a bucket and basin inside the wagon.

When we had climbed for two days and were among the snow-dusted peaks, Javier imparted some news as we rode forward to join Eleanor one morning.

'The larderer has purchased a sheep from that shepherd back along the road. He intends to spit-roast it tonight, if you approve, Princess?'

'A roast? What a good idea — that should cheer everyone up. Do you think I should invite the queen?'

He thought for a moment before replying. 'Invite her, and hope that she doesn't want to stay up late, Princess.'

I chuckled. 'Thank you, I will think about it.'

Later that afternoon, we crested a rise to find the road laid out before us, and it was all downhill.

Eleanor declared an end to our upward path. 'Tomorrow we will descend towards the Ligurian Sea, Berengaria. Let us make camp here and remember the view.'

'Indeed. My people have asked for a feast; we are having a wedding on the road soon, and they have a sheep to roast. Would you care to join us, Your Highness?'

'An *al fresco* feast at the top of the world? That might be jolly, but no thank you, Berengaria. I need my bed early these days. Who is getting married?'

I told her, and to my surprise she responded gracefully.

'Perhaps we could have another feast by the sea, when we get there. I'll contribute some victuals from my larder, perhaps.'

That night, Javier led Alazne, Arrosa and I towards a fire at the side of the track, while Karmele retired early. There was a lot of chatter and laughter from the people already gathered. As we approached, the chatter stopped, and those who had been sitting on logs and stools stood up.

'Princess Berengaria,' announced Javier.

'Please, sit and be as you were. I did not intend to disturb you,' I said anxiously.

They remained standing. Some coughed nervously, but no one sat until I was safely wedged between Alazne and Arrosa on a large log. The talking began to resume, and I felt more comfortable.

I was offered some sweetmeats, and then a table was set before me, on which there was a fine glass carafe and some goblets. Arrosa poured a drink for me.

As I looked around, I whispered, 'Where do all these women come from? I have not noticed them before.'

Arrosa laughed gently. 'Look closely. You know some, but the firelight distorts faces. Some are from Olite — your palace cooks and washerwomen. Two are the wives of a cook and the farrier, and others we have collected along the way. There are always women who are adventurous enough to latch onto a passing soldier.'

'Oh! I see. Why have I not noticed this earlier?'

'Because they are mostly following along behind us. And when you leave our little caravan, you always go forward to see the queen,' said Alazne.

'Does Father Petri know about these … liaisons?'

'He prefers not to notice, Princess,' Arrosa replied.

The noise levels had risen and wine was being passed around freely. Musical instruments appeared, and we were soon enjoying the sounds of my homeland. A shawm piped out a wail, then a *guitarra* was strummed and a tabor started the beat. Soon the musicians found their rhythm, and our fire-lit world was transformed into a festival as couples rose and began to dance.

Now I could have a conversation with Arrosa without being overheard. Javier was standing at the edge of the firelight, laughing with a couple of his sergeants.

'What has your lover said about the marriage?' I asked.

Her head spun and our eyes met. 'He is delighted, Princess! Thank you, thank you.' After some hesitant fire-gazing, she went on, 'I think that he might have been trying to ask me. For these past few days, he has begun to tell me something and then either wittered on about something inconsequential or scurried off on some pretext.' She stood up and beckoned Javier over. He wandered across the pool of firelight and stood before her.

'Arrosa?'

'We are to wed. Princess Berengaria says so.'

Javier picked Arrosa up, and turning to face the crowd with her in his arms, he repeated her announcement with volume.

A great cheer rang out that must have been heard in Eleanor's caravan.

Alazne sneaked in a gentle kiss on my cheek, and whispered, 'You are the most kind and caring of princesses.'

'We have not discussed your future yet,' I said.

'Have I got one, Princess?'

'Surely, if you wish. Worry not, you will always be close by my side. Even if I have wifely duties to perform, you will remain my companion for as long as you wish.'

There were tears in her eyes. 'It will be hard, Princess — very difficult to think of you as a wife.'

'As a queen. You will become a queen's tending lady.'

'I had not thought of that.' She smiled gently.

As if there was not enough wine to go around already, the larderer scampered off to his provisions wagon and returned with some bottles of our own Rioja.

Our celebrations resulted in another late start in the morning, but this time it was not my failing. I had left the warm log early for a good night's sleep, and I was one of the first to be up. When the rest of my people had recovered from the Rioja, we began to follow Eleanor, long gone by now. Today we were heading downward through the verdant valleys that led to the coast at La Spezia on the way to Pisa.

In the middle of the next day, the Mare Nostrum once more came into view. However, when we should have been able to see the inlet of La Spezia harbour from our position in the hills, we were caught in driving rain. It continued all afternoon and was still sweeping across us as we entered the town. There was little of interest to see, and then suddenly we were by the water and the whole caravan stopped.

I called out to Captain Javier. 'I think that I shall see what the queen has in mind. Please attend me, Arrosa. Alazne, go and see if you can find some quarters. We need to get dry.'

Arrosa and I were soon outside Eleanor's wagon. She was pleased to see me. 'Come on up, Berengaria. We haven't talked for a whole day. Are you wet? Never mind, move the cushions and sit on the wooden bench.'

I climbed inside, while Arrosa went to find shelter elsewhere. 'Good day, Your Highness. How are you now that we're back near the sea?'

'Tired, my dear, after going up and down mountains and dealing with archbishops. And we are still so far from Pisa.'

I looked at her carefully, wondering if she would survive much more of this. 'Why don't we stay here for a few days to give everyone a rest? The horses could do with one, I'm sure.'

'True. I've heard that the harbour here is quite spectacular, but I've seen little of it. A little sunshine would help, I suppose.'

'I'm sure that your people could find somewhere suitable for you to stay for a couple of days.'

She brightened up. 'Send my ladies in. I thank you for that, I feel much better now.'

Taking that as a dismissal, I was pleased to escape back to my little caravan with the good news.

Alazne had found us lodgings in a barn. We were sleeping in the loft with what little straw was left after the winter, and there was a creek nearby for us to bathe. The men were accommodated likewise in a bay further along the coast. For the staff, there were clothes to wash and mend, harnesses to repair, horses to re-shoe, wagons to service, and supplies to gather.

After a single day's rest, Eleanor was at her imperious best and summoned me for a talk. We stood at the water's edge. 'We will surely find that Richard has left us a ship when we get to Pisa,' she said.

'It hasn't happened yet, Your Highness,' I replied. 'It seems that Richard only faces forwards; what goes on behind him is of no consequence. Is this marriage something upon which he has allowed much thought?'

'Berengaria! Do you think you are of more importance than the Crusade?'

'No, Your Highness, but they are one and the same thing in time. If I find Richard, I find the Crusade, and both are missing at the moment.'

She was quiet for a moment.

'Where do you think that your galley is now?' I asked, picking up a colourful shell.

'Somewhere out there. I expect to find it at Pisa.' She looked behind her and beckoned one of her ladies to attend her. 'Bring me a chair; it is quite pleasant here.'

Once settled, she resumed our conversation, although by now I had my boots off and was knee-deep in the water.

'Berengaria,' she said to my back. I turned to face her. 'I can see that this is difficult. You have waited a long time for this marriage, and it seems to run at speed away from you. Have faith and God will reward you, of that I have no doubt.'

'Then we pray for the same thing, Your Highness. We are far from home — do you not feel cut off from all that you have known, perhaps a little lost?'

'A little,' she answered after some thought. 'Though I have made this journey before — in 1147 with my first husband, King Louis. Over forty years ago now.'

'You have been to Jerusalem?'

'No, but nearly. Perhaps you will be more fortunate than I. The whole thing was a disaster. I was sent home well before we neared the Holy City.'

'I knew about your marriage, but the Crusade has somehow been missed.'

'I don't talk about it,' she said curtly. 'But I do not have time to think of other things; there are serious matters at home. We left my other son, John, in charge of England, and he has little experience of such things. Then there is Aquitaine.'

'England! Tell me, what is England like?'

'Green, wet. The wet and green go together, it seems. And there are some fine buildings, great cathedrals … and towers.'

'Towers?'

'Yes, castle towers and the like; my husband had me kept in some. You'll know of one, perhaps: the great Tower of London.'

I'd heard something of this. 'How so?'

'A small matter. I encouraged my sons to rebel, for my late son Young Henry to take the throne. There was much discontent with my husband's rule, and I was not on good terms with him. He had a wandering eye — one of his many conquests was Alys.'

'But you had many children together.'

'Ah, yes, when we were young we lay together often, and with many a result. Beware, Berengaria: passion has a penalty. Well, enough for now. Just remember this: when you and Richard begin married life together, it is a new beginning. All that is in the past should remain there. If you can manage that, you will be off to a good start. Now, we should ensure that all is ready for the morning, so we can be on the road again!'

Eleanor stood up and departed. I sat on the sand to put my boots back on and was joined by Alazne, who had been watching from a distance and talking with Eleanor's ladies. She sat down beside me and dried my feet.

'What was that about, Princess?'

I relayed our conversation, and by the end Alazne was rolling round on the sand, laughing.

'A lecherous king, a cuckolded prince and a queen's reputation for control shattered. And this is the family that you're going to marry into?' she spluttered.

I was not amused.

CHAPTER SEVEN

The road to Pisa was quite pleasant. For two days we had the verdant hills on our left and the sea on our right, before the mighty walls of Pisa came into view. Javier went to visit Eleanor's caravan to ask about our ship.

'There's nothing there for us, Your Highness,' he admitted when he returned.

'I'll go and see what Eleanor has to say. Escort me, Javier, if you please.'

I could see that a depression had afflicted Eleanor from some distance away.

'You've heard, I suppose, Berengaria?' she said when we neared.

'Indeed: no ships.'

'There are letters, my dear — one for each of us.' She handed me a scroll that was sealed with a royal cipher.

'Does yours tell us what to do next, Your Highness?' I asked.

'Richard is in Sicily. He has Joan safe, and we are to wait here until the galley returns with further instructions.'

'How far is Sicily?'

She called over one of her captains and repeated the question.

'About five hundred sea miles away, Your Highness,' the captain replied.

'And how long ago was the galley here?' Eleanor asked.

'The harbour official told me it left about two weeks ago.'

'And how long does it take to make the voyage?'

'Two, perhaps three weeks. I think it depends on the wind and tide, though I am not a mariner, Your Highness.'

'So it might be back in another two weeks or so?'

'If they are only using the one galley, Your Highness.'

'Ah! Of course, a wise observation, Captain. Thank you, you may go.' She suddenly cheered up. 'See, Berengaria, there could be news before long.'

'Yes, Your Highness, and that itself is good news. If you will excuse me, I will go and see what news Richard has sent me.' I left before she could fashion some excuse to keep me there and share my letter. This would be the first time that I'd had direct communication with Richard since we had last met some years ago. I wanted to read it in private.

'Ahem.' Javier coughed as he walked alongside me. 'We are in a bit of a bind, Your Highness, but if we are going to be here for a while, have you spoken to Father Petri? Perhaps Arrosa and I could marry while we wait.'

'Yes, a good idea — let's have a wedding. It should cheer everybody up. I'll agree the details with Father Petri first, and then you can make the announcement.'

'Thank you, Your Highness. You are most gracious.'

'Perhaps. I only wish that I could arrange my own life so easily. Gather everyone in, and I will tell them about the shadow king.'

While Javier rounded everyone up, Alazne approached me. 'What's that?' she asked, spying my rolled-up parchment.

'It's from the king. I'll speak to our people and then … we'll go and sit on the strand.' I suddenly felt I wanted Alazne to share this. 'We can read it together.'

'Good,' she responded uncertainly.

When all were safely gathered around the back of my wagon, I climbed up a couple of steps to address them.

'You may have heard that there are no ships here to take me over the sea for my wedding, but let's use the time wisely while

I wait. Captain Javier is going to organise us into an encampment with proper facilities so that we may be comfortable for a week or two.'

'We will need a church, Your Highness,' said Father Petri.

I stepped down and beckoned Javier. 'Tell them now, Javier. If Father Petri wants a church, he might as well fill it with wedding guests.'

'Thank you, Your Highness.' He took my place on the step. 'Gather closer,' he instructed. 'You heard Father Petri: he wants a church, and he shall have one. Draw up two wagons and spread a sheet between them so that we have a covered church. Will that please you, Father?'

'Indeed, my son. Thank you, and the Lord's blessings be upon you.'

'And my betrothed,' added Javier, 'for I am to marry Lady Arrosa, and the wedding shall be in Father Petri's new church.'

That announcement was followed by a great cheer, and Father Petri's usually dour expression gave way to a smile.

I regained attention when the excitement died down. 'If you have any further suggestions, please give them to one of Captain Javier's sergeants, and we will give them some consideration. Thank you. Now, be about your duties, if you please.'

I set off with Alazne through the sparse beachside trees to find a quiet spot to read Richard's message. One of the things that Father, being an enlightened man, had insisted on, was that all of his children could read, both in our native Basque tongue and in Latin. In turn, I had insisted that my ladies were schooled in the classics and music.

As I broke off the letter's seal, my stomach fluttered. Was this a welcome or a goodbye? 'I think that he might have written this himself,' I said to Alazne. 'It does not look as if it was written by a cleric's hand. It begins: *By the grace of God, Richard, King of England, today in Messina. The tenth day of February, in the year of our Lord 1191. My dearest Berengaria, it makes my heart sad that we are betrothed to each other yet apart...*' I skimmed the rest. 'He writes lots of other nice things, then he explains that he had not enough ships suitable for a princess, soon to be Queen of England and his heart.'

'He thinks a lot about his heart. Is he ill?'

'Alazne! Desist, I am going to marry him, after all. He also writes that he has rescued his sister, Joan, got his hands on her dowry and deposed her oppressor.'

'What does all that mean?'

'It's to do with that charter Eleanor signed in Lodi; the kingdom of Sicily was in the negotiation.'

'Anything about your impending wedding?'

'No.' I sighed. 'What if I told you that I have thoughts about going back home?'

'Because you have tired of the chase? I would not be surprised. I know you too well by now, Princess: we have been pushed closer by this journey. But you are to be Queen of England at the end. Most of the princesses in Europe would happily change places with you. Has the king's letter helped you to make up your mind, Princess?'

'No. I'll wait until I meet him, then I'll make my mind up.'

Unlike most of the weddings I had attended, with all the pomp and endless speeches, Arrosa and Javier's was simple and focused on the couple saying their prayers and making their promises. A large marquee was put up, and some of the men had borrowed a large bed from Pisa and set it within this canvas boudoir for the couple's first night together as man and wife.

With the weather obliging, even in late February, the feasting went on into the night, with music and dancing around a large fire. Nobody noticed when Javier and Arrosa slipped quietly into the dark.

'Ah, well,' I said to Alazne, who was sitting by my side on one of the many logs. 'If you could leave out the bawdy talk in the morning, and let her get on with her day, it would please me. I'm off to bed. Unlace me, please, and I'll listen to the music from within my wagon.'

Three days later, I spied Javier striding along the track from Eleanor's area.

'Your Highness,' he called, 'there is news at last. There is a new galley in the harbour. It came in early this morning, it seems. The queen would like to see you.'

'Thank you, Javier. Come with me, please.'

As we set off along the road, he asked where Arrosa was.

'She is on the sand with Alazne,' I said. 'They have found a way to make necklaces from seashells. Are you both quite content now?'

'We are. Life is good.'

I laughed. 'You realise that if this galley brings the news we have been waiting for, your grand canvas bedchamber will have to come down?'

A frown passed over his handsome face. 'There is that. Have you seen inside it lately?'

'Of course not. I have not been invited.'

'I apologise, Your Highness. We are rude. You must come and see what Arrosa has done inside it. Perhaps have your evening meal with us?'

'That sounds nice. Of course I will — expect me as dark falls. Here we are.'

Eleanor's wagon was near, and she was sitting at a table in the sun giving instructions to her people, but the expression on her face was not hopeful.

'Oh, bless us,' I muttered.

'Come close, Berengaria,' said Eleanor. 'Sit with me, there are things to discuss.' She unrolled the vellum in front of her and I recognised Richard's torn-off seal lying next to it. 'Richard's fleet was delayed; most of it arrived in Messina in dribs and drabs. He has informed King Philip that he will no longer marry his sister, Alys. Philip took some convincing that the young woman had dallied with my husband, so he is not in the best of tempers. He sought advice from elsewhere and was told that it was true; Alys and Henry were bedmates. It was made worse when someone informed him that there was also likely to be a child lurking in the background, who would be his niece. Now Philip condemns my family for their immoral corruption of his sister, so he has gone off in a dark mood, bound for Akko.'

It seemed that the future of the Crusade had been put in jeopardy.

'Is there any good news?'

'Richard has promised a ship to wait for us at Napoli.'

'What about the galley in the harbour?'

'Too small for a princess and her entourage, I fear.'

'Oh, yes, I would prefer as large a ship as possible. I've not been far out to sea.'

'Unfortunately, Napoli is another three hundred and fifty miles south of here.'

Silence greeted that revelation, save for some energetic coughing from onlookers.

'Mother of God, whatever next? Will we be invited to swim to Sicily, I wonder?'

'Now then, my dear, you must be more positive. As important as your marriage is, the Crusade must take precedence. Don't you see?' Eleanor peered at me, and then seized the opportunity to address the swiftly increasing crowd. 'Prepare, prepare, my good people, for we have further to go in the service of our Lord. The affairs of men are subject to the whims of the wind and tide, but we must prevail. The Lord's business is paramount, and if we are to bask in His glory one day, we must succeed, no matter what obstacles are set before us.

'Be of good cheer, and remember the words of Pope Urban all those years ago: "You will all be forgiven for your sins on earth and save your souls if you but assist in this most holy of enterprises." So in the morning we will assist by travelling onwards and giving support to those brave men, the crusaders, at present gathering in the port of Messina with King Richard. Say a prayer and hope to join him, in due course, in Sicily.' She had risen from her seat during this eloquent homily, and indeed the people cheered her when she finished. She looked at me with sad eyes. 'Stay with us, Berengaria. Stay and see this through. I need your strength; I need your youth to help me see this venture to the end. Will you stay?'

I made a quick decision. 'Indeed, Your Highness. I will see the venture through, be assured. I should leave you now, Your Highness — perhaps you should rest.'

Halfway between the queen's camp and mine, I looked up at Javier.

'What have I done, Javier? I was offered an escape and I refused it. Forgive me.'

He halted and replied, 'Princess, you are brave and dutiful. No one could resist the call made by the queen; she has the right of it, and we must join in the discharge of the Lord's work. Do not regret your decision; you made it for all of us, and it is the proper choice.'

'Thank you, Javier. Will you stand with me while I tell our people?'

'Of course, Princess. Of course.'

PART TWO: VIEWS FROM A SHIP

CHAPTER EIGHT

The ships towered over me as I stood on the jetty at Napoli, waiting to board. The great city was set in a half-moon bay with a volcano as a backdrop. I had been shown where another city had once stood nearby, buried now under ash and rocks.

There was a great door in the side of the vessel nearest me, which was hinged down to reveal stabling inside, and men were carrying in bales of hay.

Javier strode towards me and Alazne, with Arrosa by his side, running to keep up with him. 'Captain Javier, what news?'

'All is well. Come and I'll introduce you to one of Richard's squadron commanders; he is with the queen.'

It was difficult to make our way past our wagons, all waiting to be loaded onto the ships. Javier explained the different types of vessels as we walked.

'I have been informed that this one is called a cog, common in England and Flanders. This one is a *hippagōga*, used especially for the transportation of horses. It is very slow and rolls a lot — you would not like it much. We will be speeding off to Sicily in a galley, powered by oars and sail, commonly named dromons.'

Walking further, we cleared the bulk of the cog to reveal a half-dozen oared vessels all tied up alongside each other in a raft-like formation.

'There is the commander,' said Javier, pointing to a tall, fair-haired man who was in conversation with the queen. As she saw us approach, she drew his attention to us.

Javier bowed and made the introduction. 'Princess, may I introduce Count Philip of Flanders? He is sent by King

Richard with his squadron to take you to join him at Messina. Count Philip, this is Princess Berengaria, the betrothed of King Richard.'

'Your Highness, it will be a privilege to take you over the sea. We have rigged up a galley especially for your comfort, with a canvas cabin at the stern.'

'We will not travel with you, Philip?'

'No, I shall take the lead with my vessel. It has the most oars and a bigger crew, so we shall be able to better defend you if the need arises. Your vessel shall be the second in line, so I will be in sight at all times.'

Of the vessels moored together, five were broad in the beam and seemed full of crates and boxes. The three furthest from the jetty were narrower and full of seamen and soldiers.

'What ships are these, Count Philip?' I asked. 'I think that I have seen them in sketches somewhere.'

'Your Highness is very observant. These are the type of vessels in which the Northmen came into the Mare Nostrum. The closest are *knerrir* — a single ship is known as a *knǫrr*. They are for transporting supplies. The others are *karvi*, for speed and warfare. You will travel in that *karvi*,' he said, pointing. 'It has oarsmen who can make her fly across the waves.'

'Are they slaves, Philip?'

'No, Your Highness. They are very skilled freemen, soldiers and oarsmen alike, and they cost me a lot of money.'

'How interesting. I look forward to flying across the water. How long will it take, to get to Messina?'

'When we get away, we will be off the shore of Sicily by the end of the second day. We row or sail all night — it depends on the wind.'

'How do we get over *there*?' asked Alazne, counting the hulls lying between the jetty and the outermost galley.

'There are planks from one to the next. You simply walk along them.'

We set off, dancing from ship to ship. It was precarious, especially the gaps between the hulls, which were moving. Alazne and I helped each other across.

'Your accommodation is under there,' said Philip, pointing out a tent at the back of the ship that was second from the end of the line. 'Welcome aboard, Princess Berengaria.'

'Yes, Count Philip, as you say. Can you have our requisites brought on, Alazne?'

'You are only allowed one small chest, Princess,' said Javier. 'The remainder are going on one of those big boats.'

'Well, let's pray for a swift passage.'

While we were waiting for Eleanor to make her stately way across the moving plank bridge, I went to explore with Alazne. There was a walkway down the centre of the ship. All of the oarsmen were resting, lying down underneath those hard wooden benches that I presumed they would sit on when rowing. Other crew members were busy with the sails and ropes and suchlike. There was one well-proportioned fellow at the front, who looked up and smiled as we stumbled towards him.

'Hello, ladies. Finding your feet?' He cast an eye over Alazne.

'My lady is a princess,' she pointed out.

'"Your Highness" will do, thank you. What is your position on the ship?' I asked, trying to be polite.

'I'm the steersman. I guide the vessel.'

'Is it difficult?'

'At times it is near impossible. I have to combat wind and tide with that great lever, you see?' He pointed out the steering device at the back, a thick pole which hung over the side. 'That is why I've got these great shoulders and these thick thighs.' He inspected Alazne again. 'It takes great strength.'

Poor Alazne was turning quite pink.

'Alazne is betrothed,' I said sharply.

'Sorry, Your Highness. Just making talk, Your Highness.'

'Well, don't. She doesn't like it. When will we be leaving?'

'Ah, late afternoon, Your Highness. That's when the winds are best hereabouts.'

'I see, thank you. Come, Alazne. Let's leave the steersman to his duties.'

We staggered a bit on the way back. The wind had strengthened and the vessels began to move and bang together. Someone cried out orders, and there was lots of activity at the rails. It was all fascinating, but I began to worry that I would feel ill somewhere along the way. The *komunak* was simply a canvas bucket in the tent.

Philip of Flanders took my attention next. 'Meet your ship's master, Your Highness. His name is Alek, and he is from Antwerp.'

A bearded man as wide as he was tall came to face me. He was dark-haired and he smelled of rope and tar, but he had a pleasant smile.

'*Goedendag, Prinses.* Welcome to my ship.'

'Thank you, Master Alek.'

He seemed to have run out of English, so we stood smiling at each other until Philip intervened.

'We'd best leave Master Alek to his preparations; we sail shortly. Let's see if we can make you comfortable.'

'May we stay out here? I've not sailed away before; it is so exciting.'

'Of course, we'll find you a place out of the way.'

There was a clear area behind the last rowing bench and the place where the steersman and the master stood, so Javier and I occupied it, leaving Arrosa and Alazne to sort out the accommodation.

'That's the volcano which destroyed a city, isn't it?' I asked, looking across the bay towards the smoking monster.

'Yes,' replied Philip. 'It buried the Roman city of Pompeii, though there's not much to see now. I've been here before, Your Highness. I was on the previous Crusade. We had intended to invade Egypt, but that went wrong.'

'Oh. Can you tell me a little about where you come from?'

'My father was Thierry of Flanders. He was also a crusader. He met my mother over there, and she was Sibylla of Anjou. Before she went on crusade with her father, she was married to a knight of great renown, named William Clito. He was the only son of Duke Robert of Normandy and might have been King of England one day. But fate played a hand; he died in battle and she was devastated. She told me that William remained forever in her heart, although she loved my father. I must go now; the signal that they have finished loading is flying. You are in safe hands, and we'll speak later at Messina.'

When Philip had crossed onto the outermost vessel, the boarding planks were hauled in and the crew began to take in the ropes. Then the vessels began to move — an alarming sensation.

'Look, Princess — they are raising the sail!' cried the excited Arrosa.

Sailors began to shout orders, the ship's master was pacing about the deck, and oarsmen took up their places. Ropes creaked and the sail flapped in the wind. The hull rubbed against the one next to it and made screeching noises; then there were more shouts and ropes flew through the air as they untied our ship from the next. Suddenly we were moving out into the harbour and following Philip's vessel. The wind took hold of the sail and it billowed, driving the ship forward. We were on our way to Sicily.

Eleanor came across to join me. 'All this moving about is not much different from riding in my wagon,' she said. 'What a fascinating sight.'

I looked up, intrigued by the sail and its arrangements. Then, looking down, I counted sixty oarsmen on the benches.

Turning to Master Alek, I asked, 'Why so many? Cannot one man be at each oar?'

'*Ja, gut.*' Using gestures and broken English, he explained that only one bank of men would row at a time. The innermost men would be at rest.

'I see. The steersman said that they would sail all night, but if there is no wind, the rowers will be changed?'

'They take turns, *Prinses.*'

With the bulk of that volcano on our left, we were soon near an island that climbed straight out of the sea.

'Where's that, Princess?' asked Alazne, now standing with me and enjoying the wind in her hair.

'*L'isola di Capri,*' answered Eleanor. 'It was where all the rich and influential Romans lived, away from the crowds of Rome. There will not be much to see from now on; only the coast of Italy will remain in sight until we spy the mountains of Sicily, and another volcano there.'

'Another?'

'Yes, we pass Stromboli, but on Sicily there's one named Etna, and it dominates the island.'

Eleanor went to rest, and the steersman joined in our conversation.

'When the sun drops, the wind will cease and the oars will be put to use. Perhaps you can rest until then; you might enjoy the sight of this vessel scudding through the water under muscle power.'

The fleet was sailing faithfully behind us — Master Alek often counted them, as if worried they might be swallowed up by sea dragons. Towards evening, the crew came round with meats, fruit, bread, cheese and wine. The rowers ate great platters and drank large quantities of water.

'They are getting prepared for later; they need the sustenance, I expect,' said Javier.

As dusk fell, the wind dropped, and it wasn't long before half the oarsmen stripped off for work and the rowing began. The ship's master was as good as his word; we were going to keep moving until we reached our destination.

Eleanor emerged from the tent. 'Now, my dear, we will at least be on the same island as Richard before long. I trust that he has thought to arrange the wedding. He must be busy, but if he is crossing over to the Holy Land, he will become even busier.'

'I was wondering about that, Your Highness. We have not seen each other for so long. I worry that he will not like me after all this time … or me, him.'

'Nonsense, Berengaria, who could not like you? And as for Richard, he is a king, a warrior and a crusader — a man to admire.' She became distracted as she looked down. 'Dear me, look at all those naked chests.'

The oarsmen were now illuminated by oil lamps, set in sand on the deck or hung from the mast. Muscles rippled and oars splashed to the rhythm of a drum. Alazne went into the tent, and Eleanor soon followed her.

After a while, I grew tired and Alazne showed me to a straw mattress. Everyone else occupied similar mattresses and we were quite close together, but mine and Eleanor's had curtains.

Slipping under a blanket, I listened to the sounds from outside: thump, splash. The drum had ceased, but sometimes there was a gentle call to keep the rhythm going. It was calming and it soon had me asleep.

In the morning, Eleanor's waiting woman Adelaide poked her head out of the tent and withdrew it straightaway.

'Oh, heavens!' she cried.

'What is it?' demanded Eleanor from her bed.

'The men,' said Adelaide, 'they are all hanging over the side. Some are watering the sea and others have their breeches down and are sitting on the side rail.'

'*Mon Dieu*! What are we to do?'

Someone had heard the urgent whispering, and soon Javier called in from outside the tent.

'Princess Berengaria, I'll tell you when we have cleared up out here, then pass a bucket in to you.'

'Mother of God!' cried Alazne. 'How long is this voyage to last?'

'Too long,' said Arrosa.

Javier was very discreet, handing in clean buckets filled with seawater so that we could wash ourselves.

As we headed south late on the second day, the hills on the horizon began to separate. It became clear that the mountains on our right were in fact an island.

'Sicily, *Prinses*!' called out Master Alek.

'Messina before dark!' cried the steersman.

'What happens then?' demanded Eleanor, looking at the steersman.

'We have to wait until some port official comes out to clear us for entering the port. It is well protected and we don't want a hostile reception, Your Highness.'

'What madness is this? Is not my son in command here?'

'We don't know until we get there, Your Highness. We are moving close to an area of conflict, and things change.'

Passing through the narrow gap between Calabria and Sicily, we slowed as we came close to the Messina harbour. We were not alone; in the fading light, lamps from a myriad of ships began to appear.

'This is a gathering of the invasion fleet, Your Highness,' said Javier. 'We'll have to wait until dawn to sort it out. You should try to sleep until then.'

A voice sounded across the still waters. 'Who are you?'

'Philip of Flanders!' I heard Philip reply.

'There is no room here; take your vessels across the straits to Reggio di Calabria — there is anchorage enough there!'

'Is King Richard here?' shouted Philip.

'Go away! There is no room.'

This boded ill: we were in sight of Messina yet barred from entry.

The shouting had ceased, but angry voices could be heard in the distance; Philip and whoever must have been arguing.

Nothing much happened that night and I slept only a little. At dawn, Philip's galley came alongside our vessel, and he jumped across to face us.

'There is a problem, Your Highness. Those were Tancred's officials, and they are refusing entry to the port on the grounds that it is full. They have agreed to let me ashore in order to find King Richard, but you must go elsewhere to be safe.'

'Ridiculous!' spat Eleanor. 'Have we come all this way to be turned away by some petty *officials*?'

Philip bowed his head. 'I am at a loss for words, Your Highness. I should take the offer to go ashore and let the king sort it out. You and the princess are a handsome prize if someone were to capture you. It might hamper what King Richard is trying to do: gain control of the island.'

'Capture *me*!' Eleanor's outrage must have been heard up on Etna, now visible.

Philip tried to calm the furious queen. 'The rules of chivalry only extend as far as anyone can defend them in this part of the world, Your Highness. Any scurrilous rogue can interpret them as he wishes, and Tancred has already ousted your daughter, who is now safely in Richard's possession. You must keep yourself and Richard's betrothed safe.'

'Very well,' Eleanor agreed, 'and where should we go?'

'Most of the mainland and all the ports in the south belong to Tancred, the self-styled King of Sicily. His orders will be followed. I suggest that you scud around the coast to Brindisi and take shelter there. The king will no doubt fettle this Tancred fellow and send for you.'

Eleanor looked at me. 'What shall we do, my dear?'

'It seems to me that Count Philip needs to get off and join Richard so that he is fully informed. How far is this Brindisi, Count Philip?'

'Oh, about three hundred sea miles. If they row for eight hours and do seventy to eighty miles a day, let's say it takes about four days to get there. Master Alek?'

The ship's master agreed with his estimate. He then spoke with the steersman, and Philip listened in before relaying the conversation.

'He'll get the sails up as often as he can and sail through the nights while the oarsmen rest. It might make it three days. They are familiar with Brindisi and will find you lodgings there.

I'll send word when I find out more; a horseman could cross over from one side of Italy to the other in a day. Worry not, Your Highness; it will be set to rights before long.'

Eleanor stomped off to gaze over the rail. 'Get on with it, Master Alek,' she said angrily, waving at the empty mast. 'Off you go, Count Philip. Someone should pay for this insult. Tell my son our feelings, if you will.'

'I will, Your Highness.' Hopping back over the rail, he was soon away and his galley sped off towards the harbour. Master Alek got his oarsmen into their rhythm, and we set off for the foot of Italy.

True to his word, Alek soon had us ashore and in a hostelry when we reached Brindisi. The welcome from the locals was friendly. Tancred's edicts did not mean anything over here, and as soon as they learned that the Queen and Queen-to-be of England were with them, many invitations to share a meal came our way. The nights were also warm and amenable. It was a welcome interlude, and I often slept longer than I should before wandering down to the beach to cast stones at the water.

It was the afternoon of the sixth day when a cry came from the end of the jetty. 'Ship ho!' the distant voice called. From the edge of the water, we could see a sail on the horizon.

'Is this for us?' asked Alazne.

'I pray so.' We had been expecting a horseman to come down from the hills, but a ship on the sea would suffice. Summoning my ladies, I said, 'We cannot stay here forever. My duty still awaits. Come, we will walk along to the jetty and see if this is indeed our recue vessel.'

Soon others came down to see who the new visitors were, and Arrosa and Javier hailed us as they approached.

'This looks hopeful, Arrosa. Good day, Captain Javier, how are you?'

'Well, Princess. This ship looks like the right one. Here comes Master Alek; he will soon know.'

I spied Eleanor, also on her way along the jetty. 'My word,' she said as she neared. 'Look at the size of that ship.'

It was a galley in sail, and we could see the oars flashing in the sunlight as they dipped in and out of the water. It had the wind behind it and the sails were taut. So fast was its progress that a great tumbling wave could be seen in its bows. We heard commands being issued on board. Suddenly, the sail came down and was swiftly wrapped away, the oars all came out of the water as one, and the steersman struggled with the great paddle at the back. He turned the ship around until it faced back out to sea and then came gently sideways to rest alongside the jetty, whence the crew received the mooring ropes.

'*Goed gedaan!*' cried Master Alek in admiration of the seamanship.

'*Bravo!*' shouted the large crowd now gathered, and a round of applause broke out.

By now the crew had finished all their tasks, and the oarsmen stood facing the jetty with their oars pointing skyward. The rest of the seamen were lined up alongside the boom upon which the sail was now furled, and the master was standing proudly next to his steersman to receive the tribute of the spectators. He raised an arm in salute and took a bow, much to the joy of the crowd.

'See that, Alazne? I think that we might enjoy the sail back to Messina. What say you, Your Highness?' I asked Eleanor.

'I've not seen better, I must admit.'

Alek climbed aboard and quickly returned. He went to speak to Eleanor, and I joined them.

'Your ship, Your Highness. Please go.'

Javier jumped aboard and we watched as he went to talk to the master. Soon he jumped back onto the jetty, grinning. 'The ship's master is named Calogero. He is Italian and only speaks Italian. He says that King Richard has charged him personally with your safekeeping and that we can join him at any time you wish.'

'How very kind. Berengaria?' Eleanor looked at me.

'First light tomorrow,' I replied. 'We need time to pack first.'

'Tell the master first light,' Eleanor told Javier.

'Yes, Your Highness. Can you load whatever you have tonight? It will ensure an early start.'

'Certainly.' Eleanor turned to her ladies, Adelaide and Corinne. 'Start packing and get what you can onto that ship. Does it have a name, Captain?'

'The *Volturnus*, Your Highness — god of the waters.'

'How very appropriate. And I can see that she is fast.'

'She is, Your Highness. She might take a day off the voyage, given the right winds.'

Eleanor clapped her hands, and her people scattered to get ready. I faced Alazne and Arrosa. 'We only have one chest between us. The rest is still in Philip's ship in Messina.'

'All the more time to enjoy the beach,' said Arrosa. 'I have picked some shells, see, Princess?'

'Ooh, I'd like to do some more of that,' I said. 'Come along, Javier, we're going shell-hunting. Alazne, we are going to gather more shells to turn into earrings.'

'Good, Princess. I'll help you find some.'

Javier sighed, but I was determined to spend my last night by the calm Adriatic waters in peace.

'Are you coming, Karmele?' I asked.

She was very despondent and did not enjoy life at sea. I wondered if it would be wise to take her with us much further than Sicily.

'Another ship, my princess?' she asked, clearly distressed.

'I'm afraid so, dear Karmele. Never mind, we will soon be safely back in harbour. This new ship is a beauty, is she not?'

'The ship is good, but the water does not please me. Shell-finding will take my mind off the sea for a while.'

Eventually the sun set over the hills behind us; it was near the end of March, and quite late in the evening. Alazne reminded me that we were dependent on the hostelry for food, and we should get back before Eleanor and her entourage ate the lot.

The following morning, the crew of the *Volturnus* welcomed us on board. It was tidier than the previous ship we had taken, the crew were cheery, and the decks were spotless.

Although the master was Italian, I understood him well enough. He conducted us to a wooden cabin near the back. It was in two halves with a gangway in the centre to separate them, and already Eleanor had occupied one half and was busy setting herself up. Capitano Calogero directed us to occupy the opposite side. Curtains gave us privacy. Behind the cabin at the very rear of the vessel was the open deck, from where the master controlled the steersman and the ship.

I spoke to Eleanor, for both of our curtains were open. 'Richard has done well, Your Highness, sending this fine vessel.'

'Indeed, Berengaria, although the rear of a horse has never attracted me so much since we swapped reins for sails.'

'You do not like the sea?'

'It moves too much. The short crossing from Normandy to England always filled me with dread, although the seas hereabouts seem less turbulent.'

'They can become violent, Your Highness,' said Javier. 'When the winds conspire, many a sailor has met his end in these waters.'

'Your captain is a cheerful fellow, Berengaria,' said Eleanor.

'It is in his blood, Your Highness,' I responded with a laugh.

I wanted to watch our departure and so went out onto the stern of the ship. The master gestured to Alazne and me to sit to one side and keep out of his way. Arrosa dragged Javier to the forward rail where, no doubt, she could watch the muscled oarsmen at work.

When we left the shelter of the harbour, it was clear that we might struggle with the wind. It was mostly from the side and trying to push us against the shore, but it was also very light and not much use for sailing. The oarsmen and steersman were working hard to keep us on course, and so they struggled for most of the day until the wind began to shift and they could ease off a little. They rowed all night, changing men every now and again, and it was not until daylight that some relief came for them.

That night I eventually dropped off to sleep on the tiny bunk inside the cabin — it was just off the deck, with another stacked above for Alazne.

A breeze accompanied the dawn. I awoke to a crashing noise; the ship was rising and falling, and we seemed to be scudding along under sail.

Alazne and Arrosa were gone, and Karmele seemed to be asleep. I glanced out at the rowing deck to find that the crew were having a well-earned rest. Food and wine was being taken to them, but a few were curled up under their benches, asleep.

I noted that Eleanor's curtain was closed, so I supposed her still sleeping and went up the steps to the master's deck. I found my two and Eleanor's ladies laughing and enjoying what had become a wild ride.

'Look, Princess, look behind us!' cried Alazne. She was watching over the rear of the ship. The wind was now behind us, and every wave threatened to overwhelm us. 'Isn't it exciting?'

The sail and the ropes securing it were pulling tight and loosing off as the ship ploughed through the sea. I looked forward again, seeing that all the oars were stacked and secured and the oarsmen resting. Meanwhile, the seamen were kept busy altering the sails and ropes as the master called out commands.

'Father Petri is in his favourite place,' laughed Arrosa, pointing out the cleric hanging over a corner of the rail at the very end.

'I pray that he hangs on tight,' I replied. 'Is the queen still abed?'

'Yes, Princess, she is with Corinne. She is not happy at sea,' replied Adelaide.

'And neither is Karmele,' said Alazne.

'Then they should come out here. It is better,' Javier called out. He was holding Arrosa to keep her safely on board.

Being on the master's deck was exciting once I became used to the instability. The waves came chasing up behind, then with the ship's stern lifting, the nose ploughed deep into the water, and the whole vessel twisted. Then, as the wave reached the front, the back dropped deep into the trough of the next wave. The motion was not unpleasant once I had learned to balance and sway to the rhythm of the ship.

Eleanor put in an appearance at midday without Corinne and went back inside when food began to appear. There were no prayers that day, Father Petri being indisposed.

We were heading towards the sun as it went down that evening. The wind became more violent for a while, but the master grinned and trimmed the sail to make the ship move faster. When it became dark, the wind dropped, the sail came down and we were once more under manpower. It was slower and just as noisy, but a lot steadier.

'We've got until tomorrow. You had better sleep, ladies,' said Javier.

The next time I awoke the ship was not moving, but the sounds of the morning were in evidence. Then came the ceremony of the buckets, and I hurried to try and make myself appear as a princess. Out of the one chest that we had been allowed, Alazne produced a passable gown. She then arranged my hair; a silver fillet always sat well on my dark tresses.

'Let's go out and see where we are,' she said. 'It doesn't sound as if the queen is up yet.'

Coming out into the daylight, we saw that the sea was covered in vessels of all shapes and sizes, and we were near some mountains which ran down to the sea.

Capitano Calogero was busy on deck and smiled nicely at me when I asked where we were.

'We're off the Italian coast,' he said, which left me none the wiser until he pointed at the ships between us and the island of Sicily and added, 'Messina is over there, and so is Richard.'

'Richard is still on Sicily,' I repeated to Alazne.

Then Arrosa and Javier appeared. I wondered if they had found a private space within the confines of the ship. They stared at the fleet scattered all over the sea and Arrosa exclaimed, 'Mother of God! How many ships?'

Javier took in the sight and responded, 'Thousands, my Arrosa, thousands, from all over Europe, to descend upon the Saracen armies when they arrive in the Holy Land. They'll soon give up Jerusalem when they see what God has sent.'

Capitano Calogero sent round some food, and I heard Eleanor emerge. She came to join me at the rail with a sickly-looking Corinne. We watched as various craft travelled between ship and shore.

'What are they all so busy at?' she asked, looking at Javier.

'Yes, all those boats are going back and forth like beetles on a pond,' added Alazne.

'There are many crewmen on board the ships to load stores for the journey across the sea, and perhaps shift cargoes between them. When the captains and loadmasters are happy, then the king can load his soldiers. As the harbour is full, we know that many of them will need to be carried out to those ships at anchor. So it is very busy in the Straits of Messina today,' answered Javier.

'When do you think Richard will come?' asked Eleanor. 'Ask the master, and ask him why we are here.'

Javier went over to Calogero to consult him and came back with an answer. 'He might be on his way now. See the fishermen's houses on the Italian shore? That is Bagnara; it has a tower, a *Torre*, and a monastery up on the hill. Calogero has been instructed to take us there and wait, so we will wait. We are opposite Messina, so you might be able to pick Richard's galley out among that fleet when it comes.'

I suddenly got a fluttering sensation in my stomach and said to Eleanor, 'Your Highness, there will be no time to prepare if

Richard appears suddenly. Do you think that he will like me, Your Highness?'

Eleanor stood back and looked me up and down. 'If Richard does not see the beauty in you, Berengaria, I will judge him to have gone blind. You are a sight fit for a king.'

The day was nearly gone, and I was still worrying when the man at the top of the mast cried out. He had been hoisted up there in a chair and dangled dangerously above our heads.

'The king, the king's banners, master! Thereaway!' he called, his arm pointing across the water.

'Steady, Princess. Breathe deeply and be calm.' Alazne was standing behind me. She grasped my hand.

'Thank you, Alazne,' I mumbled, but all my attention was on the fast-approaching galley.

Eight pairs of oars flashed in the evening sunlight as it sped towards us. A great standard flew from the foremast, stiff in the wind and matched by another flying at the stern.

'The royal standard and the flag of England,' said Javier.

As it neared, I picked out the figure standing at the stern. It had to be Richard.

'Do you see him, yet, Berengaria?' Eleanor asked.

I had forgotten that her older eyes might not be as sharp as mine. 'If he is broad and imperious of stature, then yes, Your Highness, I see him. He is here.'

I could hear the commands from the king's galley.

'Oars!' came the first command. 'Lift!' came the second, and the oarsmen lifted both banks out of the water, leaving them horizontal. 'Port, dip.' Those on the right side dropped the tips of their oars into the water, raising eight waves as they did. The galley spun sideways, turning around to face the opposite direction and edging closer to us. Just before the oars on the left were about to touch the side of our ship, we heard the next call.

'Lift!'

Both banks of oars were lifted as the galley nestled against the side of our ship.

'*Bene*! *Molto bene*!' cried Master Calogero in admiration of the seamanship.

The crew were about to lower a chair over the side to collect Richard when his head appeared at the rail, and he vaulted over to land on the deck with a thud in his mail armour.

'Mother!' he cried. He and Eleanor met with glee as he picked her up and twirled her around before placing her carefully back on to the deck.

'Richard!' she cried. 'Have a care — my bones are but brittle.'

'You, Mother, are indestructible.'

'Never mind me. You are here to meet another, your betrothed.'

I noticed that during this performance most people in sight of the king went on bended knee. Only Alazne and I remained standing; she was behind me with a hand on my waist for support.

Richard looked around. 'Rise up, else the waves will topple you over,' he commanded. He was about five paces away from me and now returned my gaze.

I had been examining him. He wore red hose, leather shoes, and a chain hauberk under a red chainse. This was also red and decorated with three golden lions. He had left off his helm so that his golden-red locks flowed free in the breeze, and he carried a short sword at his belt, which had a gold pommel.

I waited while he completed his examination of me. All of a sudden, the world was reduced to the small space between us. I felt Alazne poke me in the back, as if it was up to me to speak first. My stomach was churning and my knees trembled.

'Your Highness,' I ventured, and bowed a little.

'Princess Berengaria.' He returned a nod. I was glad to see that he too was a little uncertain.

'Richard. You are very tall.'

'You are very beautiful.'

Eleanor's patience was at an end. 'Oh for God's sake, Richard, embrace her.'

Richard crossed the deck and placed his hands on my hips. I stiffened as he touched me; he smelled of oils and sweat, but it was not repellent and I softened a little. 'I remember you, sweet Berengaria, yes, yes, from all those years ago.' He spoke gently so that only I and Alazne could hear. 'But you have not grown much.'

As my nose was nearer his chest than his face, this I could not dispute.

'But you, Richard, are a lot wider than I remember.'

'Ha!' Placing his hands on my shoulders, he stood back. 'The wit is still there —sharpened, I'll warrant. Are we going to joust, you and I?'

'We are going to wed, my lord,' I replied, forgetting my decision to wait before I made up my mind.

'We are? Yes, yes, we are. Mother! Come and be the first to congratulate us, for we are to be wed. The princess has agreed.'

A great cheer rent the salty air.

'Well,' said Eleanor, 'it didn't take you two long to make your minds up. Congratulations, and God's blessing be upon you … and your children.'

I looked up into his eyes and saw amusement and kindliness. He had gentle hands for one so broad.

'Are you ready to come with me, Berengaria?' he asked.

'I am — but I do not have my belongings. They were carried by one of the ships in the fleet of Philip of Flanders.' I pointed across the water towards Messina.

'I have met with Philip; he is already safely ashore.' Richard turned to his knights, who had now boarded. 'When we get back to Messina, go to Count Philip and ensure that Princess Berengaria's possessions are gathered together and brought here. At the same time, ensure that my mother's possessions are landed and taken to Castle Mategriffon in Messina.' He looked at Eleanor. 'Mother, I have a surprise for you. My galley will take us ashore here and we will visit the monastery. It is named Santa Maria of the Twelve Apostles, and someone special is waiting there.'

Standing behind Richard was a cleric, evidently an interpreter because he was given instructions by Richard to impart to Capitano Calogero. 'Tell the master, thank you, and to wait offshore. We are going to land, and I'll send him more instructions later. Do you have any more people with you, Berengaria?'

'Yes, there is Captain Javier; he is my personal guard, and he is married to my lady Arrosa, who is standing next to him. My other tending ladies are my long-term *maîtresse*, who is sitting over there, and my lady Alazne, who is behind me. The rest of my household and my fellow travellers are scattered about Philip's fleet, my lord.'

'Please call me Richard, Berengaria. Captain Javier, I welcome you. Will you be staying with the princess?'

'If it pleases you, Your Highness.'

'Of course. You've done a good job so far; you're welcome to stay. Let's get everyone ashore now from whichever ship they are on.' He turned to Eleanor. 'Can you manage to step from one ship to the other?'

'Certainly, my son. I'll be glad to place my feet on land once more.'

Richard looked over the side and hailed the steersman at the stern of his galley. It was motionless in the water but had floated a little way from the hull of our vessel. 'Bring it alongside. We are coming aboard.'

'Your Highness,' came the response. With a few commands and two or three strokes of a pair of oars, the galley was nosed into the side of our ship. I was able to step from one to the other, with Richard taking me into his arms as I stepped over the small gap between the moving hulls.

'Should I grasp you so?' he asked.

'I would think so, Richard.' I laughed. 'It might be expected of us.'

Next he turned his attention to his mother, who wore a look of determination. Stepping from ship to ship was never easy, but it was harder for those with old bones.

'Sit on the side, Mother,' Richard commanded, and she did. He watched the rise and fall between the vessels, and when they were level, he called, 'Next time!'

The next time they were level, he grasped her by the waist and placed her gently on the deck of his galley.

'Everybody aboard?' he shouted.

'Aye, Your Highness!' his steersman replied.

Within a few strokes, his craft was propelled forward at a dizzying speed.

Leaving the *Volturnus*, we sped towards the shore, cheered on by the crew of Calogero's ship. We headed towards more cheering crowds on the shore as the king's standards were recognised.

I was standing with Richard at the rear next to the steersman, and I caught a glimpse of Alazne, who was sitting on a bench at the front near Eleanor. She was sad, but managed a small smile when our eyes met.

'How many ships are here, Richard?' I asked.

'About two hundred. There were more, but King Philip of France has left for Akko with his fleet.'

'Are you and Philip on speaking terms? How are you going to manage the Crusade?'

'We've been friends for years. It'll be well — give it time.'

The royal galley was brought to a halt, gently scraping against a wooden pier. Richard handed me ashore, then helped Eleanor onto the staging. We walked together to the end, where a well-padded wagon with a donkey harnessed to it waited. I looked at it quizzically.

'For Mother,' he explained with a grin. 'But before that —' He waved to a woman on the beach. She was surrounded by armed men and a couple of monks. Seeing Richard, she stepped forward and came to greet us. Richard turned to me. 'This is my sister, Joan.' Taking Joan by the shoulder, he said, 'Meet Berengaria, my intended bride.'

Joan was half a head taller than me, with long reddish-blonde tresses, a warm smile, and startling emerald eyes. She was dressed in expensive silks, but they were plainly cut.

Eleanor let out a cry. 'Joan, Joan, my child!'

Joan smiled at me. 'A moment,' she said, going to greet her mother.

'It's been a long time,' said Richard, 'fourteen years or so. Come and meet some of my men.'

Setting off from the end of the pier, I was startled by the blare of trumpets. The crowd cheered and I was faced with an alley of lords, all resplendent in armour. Each one also wore a white surcoat emblazoned with the cross of our Lord — crusaders all.

Holding my hand, Richard conducted me between the rows of men. 'You've met Count Philip, and here are my fleet commanders, Robert of Turnham and Richard de Camville.' He continued the introductions until we reached the end of the line. He then pointed up at a building set above the beach. 'The monastery of Santa Maria of the Twelve Apostles. It's a temporary lodging; it keeps Joan safe, but tonight it shall be for all of us.'

'But it seems to be a fort, not a monastery.'

'It was built when the Norman family, the Guiscards, ruled hereabouts, to protect the monks from Islamic invasion. It's all quiet now. Let's get Mother into her wagon.'

Eleanor was soon settled, and we set off up a dusty track towards the monastery. It soon turned steep, with a deep valley to one side. Joan fell in step beside me.

'A chance to talk, Berengaria,' she said. 'I have seen you before, do you remember?'

'No, sorry. When was that?'

'When Richard first met you, twelve or so years ago. I was there, but you might not have noticed.'

'I am sorry, Joan. Still, that's a lifetime ago.'

'Perhaps, but he talked about you for a long time afterwards.'

'He did? Well, he always stuck in my memory.'

'That's hopeful. You must be in your mid-twenties now. I heard that you had taken on the duties of a queen since your mother died. Were there no suitors?'

'Plenty, but none whom I found interesting.' I was warming to Joan. 'I am twenty-five. Are you still a queen, Joan?'

'Yes, and I'm twenty-five too.'

'You must tell me all you know about your brother.'

Before Joan could satisfy my curiosity, we had reached the great iron gate of the monastery.

I had taken note of our surroundings as we walked. The building was set in a great curving gorge with seemingly no onward passage through. It was hemmed in by cliffs that reached down to the sea at each end of the bay — we could see the beach and landing jetty from up here. A watchtower sat upon the edge of a ridge. The place seemed to be isolated, both protected from the land and vulnerable to the sea. No wonder the monastery resembled a fort.

Richard was ambling up behind us, only travelling at the donkey's pace to keep his mother company. Arrosa and Alazne caught up with us, and I introduced them to Joan.

'You are well served, I see, Berengaria,' she smiled. 'I will introduce you to my tending ladies, Pavot and Torène, when we are settled.'

'How gracious, Joan. Arrosa is married to that handsome man walking in front of your mother's wagon.'

'Ah, I see. How do you find him, Arrosa? Is he gentle?'

'He is, Your Highness. He's all I could wish for.'

'And you, Alazne, are not married?'

'No, Your Highness. I serve my princess.'

We waited outside the gate while everyone caught up with us, and then Arrosa asked Javier, 'You fell behind, my love — why?'

'I wanted to speak to one of the king's officials about our chattels and such. We might catch up with them one day. Are they going to open that enormous gate?'

The small postern gate at the side opened slowly, and a wizened old monk poked his head out.

The king hailed him. 'Brother Michel, we are safely arrived.'

The monk stepped out. He wore a brown habit, and a toothless smile lit up his face. 'Your Highness,' he croaked, 'welcome. You have brought some more ladies for safekeeping.'

'I have. Could you harbour them for a few days? I will be leaving on the morrow. I'll be back soon, but I must get off to join King Philip before he wins the war unaided. Unlikely, I know, but I shan't take the chance of being left out.'

As Richard went back to help Eleanor out of the wagon, Brother Michel waved us inside. 'You know where to go, Your Highness,' he said to Joan.

'Indeed. Are we all in the same lodgings?'

'Yes, we have no other visitors today. Pick your own cell.' He then turned his attention to the male members of our party.

Joan led us across a courtyard to a long, low building on the opposite side. Inside was a long corridor with a dozen doors leading off.

'Pick a chamber,' said Joan. 'I'm in here.'

She opened the first door to reveal a bed and a wash basin on a chair. A crucifix decorated one wall and opposite was an icon of the Holy Mary.

'What now?' I asked.

'If you take your ladies down to the far end and fill the cells up from there, I can get Mother in the cell next to me. Is that fair?'

'Good, thank you. I hear them approaching now. I want to talk to Richard. I'll get Alazne and Arrosa into their chambers and find him.'

'I'll come with you. There are only two places where men and women can meet: the chapel and the refectory, for meals.'

We went over to the refectory and Richard was there. I noticed that when we entered, the monks crept out, leaving Brother Michel to manage on his own.

Richard broke off talking to his men and greeted us. 'Sorry about that — got a war to plan. Now then, Berengaria, shall we take a walk?'

'I'll stay with Mother,' said Joan. 'We've lots to catch up on.'

There was a frugal display of food on a buffet table, so I grabbed a bite of cheese and bread. There was no wine, only water. Then Joan gathered Queen Eleanor and her ladies and headed off towards the visitors' block.

Richard looked over my shoulder at Alazne and Arrosa. 'Are they coming?'

'Leave us, if you please,' I said to my ladies. 'We'll not be long.'

'How about a stroll down to the beach?' said Richard. 'There are too many ears hereabouts.'

I agreed, but when we stepped outside, the sun had gone. 'It's turning dark — will we be safe, Richard?'

'Yes, I can't go anywhere without an escort; my commanders will not allow it.' He indicated three shadows. 'A captain and two sergeants, the best. There's a bit of a moon; we'll be safe.' He opened the postern gate to allow me to step through.

As we moved off, our escorts emerged from the shadows to follow.

It was a pleasant night. Any cloud had cleared and the moonlight was reflecting off the sea. Richard's galley, moving gently on the water, had its masts lit up by the moon; it was a very pretty sight.

'Nice night,' offered Richard. 'I don't get the chance to look at such things much. I've been thinking about you, though. Memories play tricks — you're different somehow.'

'I can remember you as I saw you when I was twelve. Such stories that are told about you now aren't suitable for a twelve-year-old.'

We reached the sand near the end of the pier. I picked up a stone to skim it in the moonlight.

'You have doubts?' he asked.

'I trawled through doubts all the way here, Richard. But I came because I can still remember the first time that we met. I was curious to see how you had changed. Have I changed? What made you persuade your mother to drag me across Europe?'

He faced me. I felt the weight of his hands heavy upon my shoulders. 'We shall be honest. I simply do not have time to waste. Is that the first thing which we may agree upon?'

I watched his eyes and felt his tension; he did want this. 'Yes, Richard, that is the first thing we can agree on. I did not come here to fail in any purpose. I felt an attraction all those years ago…'

'You have it right, Berengaria. Mother does have a role in this, which must be obvious, but it would not work if you were not agreeable, nor if I found you…'

'Ugly?'

'Yes, I can't be doing with ugly princesses.'

'Nor I with prevaricating kings.'

We had our first laugh together; this was hopeful.

'Then we are agreed to try and make a marriage work?'

'We are.'

'Shouldn't I kiss you?' he asked.

'A kiss will suffice for now.'

The three shadows on the beach coughed and moved away, and I had my first taste of the man I was destined to marry.

CHAPTER NINE

Richard said goodnight and kissed my hand outside the women's cells, leaving me to ponder how I felt as I walked along the corridor.

Alazne and Arrosa were sitting on the bed when I entered.

'Princess?' said Alazne uncertainly. I went to her and kissed her on the forehead.

'Do I get one, Princess?' asked Arrosa.

'Of course, I love you both dearly.'

'But there's going to be a wedding,' burst out Alazne, and she began to cry.

I sat down between my two ladies, and they rested their foreheads on my shoulders.

'Now then, you know why I travelled here. There are duties that must be undertaken.'

'Yes, Princess,' sniffed Arrosa, 'but we might be split up.'

'No, that will not happen. Now, off you go. I'll see you in the morning. God bless.'

I woke early. 'Hello, ladies, are you awake?' I called, my voice echoing down the bare corridor.

'Just, Princess,' answered Arrosa from next door.

'What shall we wear? All of our belongings are spread across the king's fleet,' moaned Alazne, still unhappy.

'Come in here, my sweet,' I said. She came into my cell wearing only her nether breeches and a shirt that was hanging open. 'Do not fret so. Things have a way of working themselves out.'

'I suppose we'll have to wear what we came in.'

We dressed and went past Eleanor's cell on our way out. I bade her good morrow, but her ladies were struggling to get her ready and I received a gruff response. When we entered the refectory, we found Brother Michel, Richard and his entourage.

'Come join me, Berengaria,' said Richard. 'There's fresh fish and bread and some scabby apples from last year. I need to tell you something — isn't that so, Brother?'

Brother Michel nodded and smiled.

'We can't get married here — it's Lent! Marrying is not allowed. We must re-arrange. I'm taking Mother over to Messina to send her home. I received word about that knavish brother of mine, John, making a mess of England. Mother is going to sort him out. Will you and Joan — here she is — stay here? I'll send a ship for you — women can't travel with the men, you know — Crusade etiquette. Joan, I want you to come with Berengaria to the Holy Land.'

Joan sat next to me on the bench, gave me a kiss on the cheek and agreed to Richard's plan.

Eleanor arrived with much fuss, and Richard explained the situation.

'I must take my betrothed to Akko, Mother. We can't get married here during Lent.'

'I don't want to go to Akko. I need to get back and bring your brother under control. He's losing the support of his nobles.'

'I've arranged it, Mother. I'm taking you over to Messina; there's a fast galley there to take you back north.'

'Good, but not too far by sea, Richard. I prefer my chariot.'

Having finished my breakfast, I decided to go outside to clear my head. 'Will my ladies come with me, please? I need to do some thinking.' As I stood, I said quietly to Joan, 'When you've finished here, would you join us by the water's edge, please?'

She nodded and then went to sit next to her mother. I wondered if they were planning something interesting for Prince John.

Javier was waiting outside with a pair of sergeants, and we set off down the hill. When we reached the beach, I sat down on the sand to remove my shoes.

'We've come this far, Javier,' I said. 'It's time to decide if you want to go any further. The next voyage will take us away from this shore and very far from home. You might never return if you come with me.'

I stood and hitched my skirts into my belt so I could paddle in the sea. Meanwhile, Alazne, Arrosa and Javier had a frantic discussion. Karmele wandered across the sands and joined them.

Eventually, they broke up and approached me.

'We might have a decision, Princess,' said Alazne.

I looked at them. Alazne was holding Karmele's hand, and Javier was holding Arrosa's.

'What is it?'

With tears in her eyes, Karmele answered, 'They will remain with you, Princess. I cannot; this galloping across the world has left me quite dizzy. I would like to return to Olite, and I know that some of your entourage would like to return too.'

'Ship or horse, if you want us we'll stay with you, and most of the other servants from your Olite palace,' said Arrosa. 'But as Karmele says, some want to return, as they are too fond of home to travel any further.'

'I see.' Tears welled in my eyes, but I needed to test their resolve. 'If you stay, I'll hear no complaints, nor accept responsibility for your decisions. If you understand that, I would count myself privileged to have you travel with me.'

Alazne, Arrosa and Javier charged into the water and embraced me.

Then I became aware of a shadow on the beach and looked around to see Joan watching with an expression of total astonishment.

'I am glad to join you on the journey to Akko,' she said. 'Sicily is a realm of loneliness; I have never been happy there. I was an asset to expand Father's influence, and Mother colluded in that, but I was never asked if I was happy. I am glad to leave it all behind me and seek out my destiny elsewhere.'

'I am very pleased to have you with us, Joan. Will you bring your own tending ladies?'

'Of course, if I may,' she replied. 'Pavot and Torène are nice young women.'

I waded out of the sea and took Karmele by the hand. 'I am so sorry,' I said. 'I should not have asked you to come so far.'

'Oh, Princess, I love you dearly. I had hoped to go to Jerusalem to be shriven, as you know, but it is too distant. There comes a time when the old must part company with the young, and it is best done with dignity. Besides, who will regale your father's court with stories of our journey, if it is not to be me? Go, my love. Go with my blessing and take all our happy memories with you.'

'I can arrange for you to travel with Queen Eleanor, along with anyone else who wishes to return. You will be safe with her.'

We embraced, and I noticed how frail my old nurse's body had become.

'God bless you, dear Karmele. And remember that those who *help* in this sacred Crusade shall also be granted remission of sin, even if they don't reach the Holy City.'

'What a waste, for I have not committed any sin to forgive.'

We laughed, and then I turned my attention to practical matters. 'Javier, send someone back for Karmele's things. She will be leaving with the queen very soon.'

Later that day, we stood on the pier and watched an assortment of people on their way to board Richard's galley. The king was walking alongside Eleanor, who was seated in a donkey cart.

'Berengaria, Berengaria, my dear!' she called. 'Do come and give your new mother a hug. I am being sent off again.' When I reached her side, she went on, 'Now, give me a kiss and let us go our separate ways. I shall see you in Aquitaine when Richard has finished his Crusade or before next Christmas, God willing.'

'Thank you, Your Highness. I admire your resilience and thank you for your guidance. I have learned a lot, especially about dealing with Mother Church and her politics.'

'Quite. Just remember to try and find out what lies behind what folk say before you agree to anything.'

'Come along, Mother. There's much to do today,' said Richard. He cast a leg over the rail of the galley. Eleanor and Karmele were each seized by the waist and pulled onto the ship.

Turning to me, Richard said, 'A ship will be with you before the week is out, Berengaria. Farewell.'

'Not yet, Your Highness. Before you depart…' With one foot in the galley and one on the pier, I grasped him by the shoulders and planted a kiss on his lips. He nearly fell into the gap before stumbling onto the deck.

Eleanor laughed and gave me a wave.

The ship's master gave some orders and soon the galley was speeding across the sea towards Messina. My last view was of Eleanor holding Karmele around her shoulders to comfort her.

Alazne caught my eye and shyly asked for a talk. Joan, Arrosa, Javier and the rest of the witnesses were clearing off the beach now.

'We'll catch you up later,' I called to Arrosa. 'We're going for a walk.'

Soon the pier was clear, so instead of walking I sat down on its edge. 'Sit next to me,' I said to Alazne. 'Are you worried about what lies ahead?'

'Yes, Princess, it's all happening very quickly. But could you stop it here, if you wanted? We could both return to Olite.'

'I want my chosen path more than ever, now that I am re-acquainted with Richard,' I said, looking into her eyes.

'After two days?' She sniffed and a tear ran down her cheek.

I placed an arm around her shoulders. 'After twelve years of waiting.' I kissed her cheek. 'We will run with the stream and see where it takes us. That is all that I can promise.'

She nodded. 'That's all I can expect, I suppose.'

We stood and made our way back up to the monastery. Two of Javier's sergeants appeared from behind a fisherman's hut at the edge of the beach and fell in behind us.

When we returned, Javier said that he had secured a bathing chamber for us. 'The monks only use it four times a year for the full douche, before the major feasts in the calendar. I'll have my men fill the tubs for you. There's one hot tub and one cold. You can make use of them, and we'll stay outside.'

I waited until dark. The hot tub was steaming when we entered, and Alazne, Arrosa and I were soon relaxing in the water together.

'How long will it take to get to Akko, Princess?' asked Alazne.

'Who knows. How far is it?'

'Javier says that it is beyond a thousand miles,' Arrosa answered.

'A long voyage, my ladies,' I said.

After four more days at the monastery, an excited monk ran into the courtyard to tell us that a ship had been spied.

We ran down to the beach. When the ship had been secured, a bearded man came down from the raised part at the stern of the ship and leaned over the rail.

'Anybody know the whereabouts of Princess Berengaria?'

'I'm Princess Berengaria, and over there is Queen Joan of Sicily,' I said.

'Oh … begging your pardon, Your Highness. We're here to take you to Akko, if you please.'

Joan was by my side now, so I asked her opinion.

'Is this one suitable? Has Richard served us well?'

She looked up at the ship towering over the pier. It was much larger than Richard's galley. 'What are you carrying, Master…?'

'I'm William, William of Harfleur. We are carrying supplies for the army.'

'A Norman master,' Joan said to me. 'We should be safe with him.'

'Have you got a privy closet on there?' demanded Alazne.

'Aye. The vessel is named *Dione*. The king made us build a closet before we came to you, especially for the ladies. There are bunks too.'

'Very well,' I answered, 'you may take us to Akko … in this goddess of the sea.'

'I'll find your things,' said Javier.

'Well, that won't take long,' said Arrosa with a wry smile. 'There must be hundreds of ships out there.'

'About two hundred, my lady,' said William.

It took two more days and a tour of the ships at anchor close to Messina before we were united with our chests, and everything in them was damp.

CHAPTER TEN

'What day is it, Javier?' I asked once we were on board the *Dione*.

'The tenth day of April in the year of our Lord 1191, Your Highness.'

'This is a glorious sight.'

'Over two hundred ships, all headed to the far horizon, Your Highness,' said William of Harfleur.

'And thousands of men,' added Arrosa.

We were slow and behind most of the ships in the huge fleet, partly because this lumbering giant couldn't match their pace.

'What do we do now, Joan?' I asked.

She shrugged. 'Have you brought anything to amuse us?'

'I have some needlepoint in a chest somewhere,' Arrosa offered.

Father Petri, from his usual place near the rail, looked up. 'I can do readings from the scriptures, Your Highness.'

'Ah,' I said, 'you have the scriptures and a Bible?'

'Indeed, and the epistles.'

'Then we shall practise reading,' I said.

'I've got books on navigation, Your Highness. I can teach you that as we go along,' said Master William.

That was the best offer I'd had, so I agreed. But to remove the sour expression from Father Petri's face, we also agreed to attend his scripture sessions.

Once we left Messina behind, the mountains of Sicily began to fade from view, so we could only see those of mainland Italy on our left. The fleet was separating now; the fast galleys were only just visible on the horizon, while the slow cargo vessels gathered near each other behind. I asked Master William if Richard had it in mind to gather the whole fleet together from time to time.

'Aye, Your Highness. We have orders to make for Crete, then Rhodes, before by-passing Cyprus and heading for Akko. That way, the warships will always be at the fore, and we shall amble along behind but remain in touch.'

'Thank you, William, and thank you for our quarters.'

'I should make a tour of the ship now that we are underway. If anyone would like to accompany me, I shall explain how the vessel works and who does what along the way.'

We all agreed and went exploring with Master William.

The front was the bows, where the crew had an open-air closet. The right-hand side was starboard, where the steering oar was, and the opposite side was where they could bring the vessel alongside in a port without damaging the steering oar, although this ship had a rudder at the rear — or the stern, to use its proper name. The hold was full of crates of arrows — and at the very back, next to a hatch, sat our chests of clothes.

The master and the steersman occupied the afterdeck, beneath which our living spaces had been fashioned. These were tiny cabins with a gangway running between the two sets of berths, four in each, two on the deck and two high above them. But, except for canvas screens, the sides were open to the wind and sea.

The second full day was Good Friday, and we spent it in contemplation. By day three I was feeling comfortable, although Father Petri showed no signs of leaving his favourite place hanging over the side. I felt sorry for him and thought that I might drop him off at the first port of call.

By late morning there were portents in the air, and Master William seemed worried when I went up to see him. The sky in the west, astern of us, was heavy with black clouds and the wind was pushing the bow into the water. As the stern was raised up, the ship twisted and plunged. It was most uncomfortable.

'Doesn't look good, Your Highness,' he said. 'We need to prepare for a storm. Have you anything to wear apart from your kirtles?'

'Yes, we have riding apparel.'

'Can you swim, Your Highness?'

'Only if I can touch the bottom.'

'You won't do that out here. My advice is to wear breeches and no shoes. And if it gets really bad, we will rig hand lines along the deck and tie straps to your waist so that you can tie yourselves to them. My crew are going around the ship now to ensure that everything is properly secured. Bring your people out and shelter in front of the cabin; they will feel less nauseous in the open and won't be trapped if the worst happens. And please hurry; that storm is catching up with us.'

The clouds behind the vessel were lit by flashes, as if God were moving a lantern inside them. I rushed down into the cabin to get everyone into less cumbersome clothes and get them up onto the deck.

'Why does this ship wallow about so much, Master William?' I asked when I returned to his side.

'It is the cargo, Your Highness. There are many barrels and crates, but they mostly contain arrows, which are very light compared to our normal cargoes. The ship does not sit down in the water, and so we are like a wine cork in a tub.'

'It's horrible. Can't we turn around?'

'Most definitely not!' William shouted above the wind. 'She'll broach if we turn, and if we did manage it, we'd batter into the waves and they'd come straight over the top. Believe me, Your

Highness, I've done this before; to run before the storm is the safest way.'

'Then why does this ship have no oars?'

'They take up cargo space, Your Highness, and the turbulent sea would smash the oars and throw oarsmen about. Now, I need you all to keep the afterdeck clear. Go down the steps and shelter there in front of the cabin, but do not go into it, for safety's sake. I need at least three men on this rudder to hold it against the power of the waves.'

I crept down the steps, clinging to the handrail, and staggered across the deck to join the rest of the passengers sheltering in the lee of the cabin.

'What is to happen?' asked Joan. 'What did Master William tell you?'

'Lots of things. Let's sit down in the corner here.'

Wedging ourselves in against the front of the cabin, we got into a huddle. I had Alazne and Arrosa on my left, and Joan was with Pavot and Torène on the right. Javier stood by the rail, keeping an eye on Father Petri, who was all but comatose now and retching blood.

'We are in trouble!' I shouted above the wind. 'The ship is at the mercy of the wind. We must keep some sail up so that the rudder can work, but we cannot go back in case a wave breaks against the side and turns us over, so the only way is forward. The cook has doused the fire, so there is no warm food.'

'What happens when it gets dark?' shouted Joan.

'Master William says that they will hoist a lamp up the mast, and we will see if there are any other ships near us. We should try and steer close to the others.'

We sat watching the daylight fade and feeling sick. The cook came by, staggering from handhold to handhold, and hurriedly introduced himself as Stephen of Fécamp. He gave us a gourd filled with water, and a crewman handed over a couple of damp loaves.

Just before it turned dark, the wind eased a little and two seamen came to us with a canvas sheet and secured it across our bodies, lashing it down with ropes. It provided a little relief from the cold, and we huddled closer.

Sometime during the night, Javier staggered across the deck and bellowed into my ear. 'Father Petri has gone!'

'What, overboard?'

'No, he has died, Your Highness. He kept repeating, "We have missed Easter Sunday", though it is not until the morning.'

'We'll pray for him now,' I said. 'Secure yourself, Javier. Come under here and hold Arrosa; she is terrified.'

The morning brought light, but no respite from the wind. To deepen our despair, it also brought rain, which streamed down our backs, unhindered by the canvas. I decided to stand up and face the day.

There was a crack and a flash, and the lantern at the top of the mast exploded, hit by God's hand. The debris landed on the deck, and the rope holding it up landed on a seaman, knocking him down.

I rushed to his side with Joan. He lay moaning, with a gash in his head. The ship wallowed and we three slid across the deck into the rail.

'Hold on here,' I cried, terrified that I would be washed overboard, and Joan held me with one hand and the rail with the other. The injured seaman slid across the deck to join us. 'Tie our safety ropes to something!' I called as I held a hand to the gash in the seaman's head.

Master William had seen the incident from the afterdeck and sent two crewmen to help. Then, between the worst of the ship's sideways movements, we slid the man along the deck and into the corner, where we had been sheltering.

He struggled to sit up, and although still dazed he appeared to be in good spirits.

Alazne disappeared into the cabin and came back with some lengths of cloth — torn from a good gown, I noticed. She wound the man a turban to keep his wound covered.

'We should find some canvas and fashion a shroud for Father Petri,' I reminded my friends. 'Javier, go up to Master William and see what we can do about his body.'

'Your Highness, I think that they slip bodies over the side, committing them to the deep and the Lord's mercy. I'll go and check when it calms down.'

We entered a calm period later in the morning, and Master William was able to survey the *Dione* for damage. He sent a seaman up the mast to rig another lantern.

'We'll need it for tonight, so it's best to do it now,' he told me.

'Can you see any other vessels from up there?' called Joan.

'Aye, half a dozen ahead of us on the horizon.'

I watched Javier and the ship's sailmaker stitching up poor Father Petri's shroud. 'It's a watery grave for him, Joan. God bless him.'

Suddenly, there was a scream and the seaman hurtled down from the mast and crashed onto the deck, followed by the new lantern and its new length of rope.

Master William sped down from the afterdeck, shouting, 'Where's the leading seaman? Where's Jacob?'

'Here, master.' A burly crewman stood up from inspecting the body, shamefaced.

William put his face close to Jacob's. 'Who is it?' he demanded.

'Denijs, master.'

'Why wasn't he secured, eh?'

'He was, master,' replied Jacob.

'Show me the rope,' ordered William.

'It's still up there, tied where he tied it himself.' Jacob pointed up the mast.

'Who secured it to his waist?'

'I did, master. It was very busy.'

'Well, busy yourself with this,' William replied. He let fly an almighty blow that landed Jacob on his back. 'Consider yourself no longer my leading seaman, and your pay this month will go to Denijs's family. I know them well. Now, go and work for the cook until I decide what to do with you.' He looked at us. 'There's no room for sloppy work at sea, Your Highnesses. We all have to look after each other. Someone on deck should have watched Denijs secure the rope and tested it before he committed his life to it. And if you look behind you, you'll see why.' He turned to his crew. 'Back to your stations! The storm is upon us again. Get Denijs's body secured; sailmaker, another bag, if you please. Ladies, secure yourselves again.'

When the light began to fade the wind eased off, I came out of the canvas to ease my stiff bones.

'Are you coming, Joan, Alazne? Let's visit the master,' I said.

Arrosa and Javier were still curled up, sleeping.

Poking my head above the afterdeck steps, I called, 'May we come up, master?'

'Have you got waist ropes on?'

'Yes.'

'Come up and tie yourselves onto the safety rope. We've entered another quiet area. It can come back, though.'

'Do you know where we are?' asked Joan.

'Ha! East of Sicily and West of Constantinople is my best guess, Your Highness. The only thing I know for sure is that there are three more ships ahead of me.'

'What shall we do?' asked Alazne.

'When things calm down, I can consult my charts and my needle.' He held up a box and opened the lid; it had a metal pointer inside that seemed free to spin about. 'We have been heading a little south of east for so many hours. Then I can estimate the speed at which we have been moving, and I'll have an idea of where we are … within a hundred miles or so.' He laughed. 'If it continues to abate, I can let you go down below to see if you can sleep.'

'Thank you for your seamanship, William,' I said. 'The king shall hear of this.'

'Thank you, Your Highness, it's my job. Don't forget that we have two burials to perform.'

'No, I have not forgotten. Do you have your own Bible?'

'Indeed. You want me to do a reading from it?'

'If you would.'

The afternoon was grey with some lightning flashes on the horizon, but the wind continued to abate — just the dismal atmosphere for funerals.

William read from the Bible, and we prayed together before the ship's carpenter released the bodies from a board he had prepared for the occasion. We watched them slip into their watery grave. Before the light faded, William allowed us down into the cabin.

It smelled damp and the water had seeped into our bedding, but the *Dione* was more stable now. We were so tired that the space was more welcome than another night up on the windswept deck. I warmed my wet mattress with my body, trying to forget the days now behind us.

The next morning was a lot warmer.

'Good, now we can dry off,' I said to the others. 'Can we get screens up and stop those men from wandering back and forth? I don't know what they find to do at the back, but they seem to find it interesting.'

'They keep looking down that hatch,' said Joan.

I climbed up on deck, then up to William's position next to the steersman. It was a beautiful day: the sea was calm, the sun was shining, and the ship's progress was gentle.

'*Goedemorgen*, Your Highness, and anybody else who can lend a hand,' Master William greeted me as I climbed the steps to his afterdeck, followed by Joan and Alazne.

'What needs doing, master?' I asked.

'Your cabins, for a start. Throw out the bedding and lay it on the deck to dry in this sunshine. Then there is a hatch in the deck down there; we need to go down it to get to the bilges, which lie between the cargo deck and the hull. The bilges will be full of seawater, and we need to bring it out, bucket by bucket. I'll send a man in there and he will fill buckets and hand them up to you. If you would help by forming a chain with your ladies, you can pass the buckets along and tip the water over the side. In the meantime, Stephen — the cook — can get his fire going, and we'll have a hot meal before midday. Then, if all is well, I'll allow you some fresh water for your hair.' He grinned. 'And you may empty your chests of clothing and lay it on the deck to dry before you grab a bucket.'

Joan laughed. Her hair was matted, her face was white with salt, and her clothes were rumpled. I knew I looked the same.

The bedding came out of the cabin, followed by our wet gowns. Then the hatch went up to reveal a dark space full of slopping water. The smell was foul, and I felt sorry for the seaman who was ordered down there to fill the buckets — it was Jacob, and he did not complain.

I was not sure how long we worked, handing up bucket after bucket, but when Master William was satisfied he called a halt. The sun was going down, so we brought in our tattered collection of gowns.

'Well done, ladies, Your Highnesses — you have all performed well. I was a bit surprised when you agreed to work,' said William.

'My hands are ruined,' moaned Arrosa. We laughed and joined in with her lament.

Smiling, William shouted down the hatch and ordered that a casket of sheep's wool be brought up. While he waited, he was pleased to announce, 'Stephen has also done well. If you gather on the main deck, he has prepared a few things for you. Perhaps I can allow a modicum of wine in return for your efforts … and you can all have two buckets of fresh water for your own use. Use it wisely, for we might still be two or three days from land.'

The wool arrived in a salt-encrusted container.

William broke it open and invited me to inspect the contents. 'So, do your soldiers put this to good use, Your Highness?'

'Indeed they do,' I said. 'It keeps their weapons bright and rust-free.'

'And their hands?'

'Of course, their women swear by it; the oil on the wool keeps their skin soft and supple. Thank you, Master William. We'll use it after we've been fed, if we may.'

Later, we sat back against the rail, eating our hard-earned repast: fresh bread from Stephen's oven, muslin-wrapped cheese from somewhere cool inside the ship, and a cup of pottage. It had chopped root vegetables and some dried meats floating in it.

'What next, Master William?' I called across the deck.

'We carry on, Your Highness. Those ships in front have slowed down; soon we shall be together as a fleet. One good thing about the Mare Nostrum is that if we keep going for long enough, we will see land — it is just a question of whose. Meanwhile, we will get on with repairing the vessel where it may be damaged. From experience, I believe the worst of this storm has passed. As for what happens next, it is in the hands of God, but now we make the best of what we've got.'

CHAPTER ELEVEN

As the fleet drew closer together, it became obvious that some of the vessels had not escaped the storm as lightly as we had. I was on the afterdeck as Master William examined our fellow voyagers.

'See that one, Your Highness? It has only half a mast,' he said. 'We should all now be searching for land in order to repair the damages. See that ship furthest away, near the horizon? He has a man at the top of the mast, looking out. We'll close in on him if we can.'

He gave orders, the sails were reset and we began to move through the water with greater speed.

Screwing up his eyes as we neared the other vessel, Master William declared, 'If I'm not mistaken, that ship is most important and should be closer to the king's centre than it is.'

'Why?' I enquired.

'It should be carrying the Keeper of the King's Seal, Roger Malcael.'

'Is he not the vice-chancellor?' asked Joan.

'Indeed. They are well off course, as are we,' confirmed William.

Over the next few days, the leading ship slowed to the speed of the most damaged ship.

'As we have lost the main fleet, we might as well stay together. The next land we spot will decide what we do next,' William informed us.

With the sea calmer now, we became accustomed to the gentle rolling of the vessel. It was almost dark when there was a hail from the masthead of the leading ship.

'Land, on the port bow!'

Soon everyone was on deck, and Joan and I were allowed up on the afterdeck with Master William.

'Where is it?' I asked.

'I can't be certain, but from the lie of the land and my charts, I shouldn't be surprised if that was the island of Cyprus.'

'Are we going to land there, Master William?' asked Joan.

'Not tonight. See that headland on our port bow? It protrudes about a mile from the mainland. There are castles on either side, according to my map; one is named Kolossi and the other is Lemesós. We will round the headland and find shelter in the bay on the far side. I'll drop anchor and wait until morning. We have orders to stay off the coast, as the king is not certain about the ruler of the island.'

'Who is that? Who will not aid crusaders?' I asked.

'He's a fellow named Isaac Comnenus. He is of the family who rule Byzantium from Constantinople,' said Joan. 'He has named himself the Emperor of Cyprus, which is a bit high-handed.'

'Yes, Your Highness — an island is hardly an empire,' said William. 'We'll remain offshore until I work out the situation. Meanwhile, we will set sentries and you can all settle down for the night when we are safely at anchor.'

We scampered down to the working deck to watch the anchors being prepared.

The island loomed dark on the left and we crept along with minimum sail set. William said that he hoped that the other vessels ahead had good control, else they could run aground.

He had a man in the bows, throwing a rope into the water. It had a lead weight on the end, and by the amount of rope that paid out, he could tell how deep the water was. 'Fifteen!' he called out. Then he pulled the rope in to hurl it ahead once more. 'Ten!'

'Ten what?' Arrosa asked.

'Paces,' answered Javier. 'The rope has a knot every pace; he is counting knots.'

When 'three' was called, William shouted, 'Loose!' A crewman tugged on a rope, the anchor fell into the sea and we came to a halt. By now we could see people on the beach.

'There's a harbour there, look.' Javier pointed it out. I could just make out the shadow of a tall building seemingly sitting in the water.

'What is that?' I asked.

'It's a pharos; it'll be on the end of a pier, the entrance to the harbour, and it should be lit. They might not be expecting us, or they're trying to wreck us on the beach. Morning will tell.'

It was still dark when I woke. I could hear shouting and banging out on the deck and I became worried.

'Quickly, clothes on,' I said to Alazne.

At that moment, a shout came down to us from the deck. 'The master says to get up, ladies! There's something going wrong ashore.'

Joan was the first to scamper off up the steps and Arrosa was next, both having slept in their clothes, it seemed.

I emerged from the cabins to find Joan above me on the afterdeck. 'Come up, Berengaria. There's fighting on the beach.'

William and a couple of his crewmen were hanging over the rail, trying to see what was happening. It was just turning light.

I hurried up to stand behind them. 'What can you see, master?'

'Your Highness, two of the early ships have arrived on the beach; they must have lost control or not been sure how far offshore they were. Now they are under attack — just what I feared. It is serious because Vice-Chancellor Malcael is in one of them.'

'Master!' A seamen was pointing. 'Those Griffon soldiers are leading the crew away from the ship — looks like they've got their hands tied behind them. Prisoners, they are, prisoners.'

'What're Griffons?' I asked.

'The Byzantine Greeks,' explained Joan. 'They rule Cyprus, which is a pottage of various people.'

'Are they Isaac Comnenus's people?' I asked.

'He is the ruler of Cyprus, so yes.'

'What will we do, Master William?'

'Wait. I can see a fort over there, about two hundred paces from the harbour; that must be Lemesós Castle. We could haul up the anchor and go back out to sea, but I'd rather stay here, where we can see more. I'll send a boat across to our other two ships at anchor over there, and see what they think.'

'And then?' asked Joan.

'We'll wait and see if any more ships turn up. Perhaps the king will find his way here. I'm going to rig up some netting along the side of my vessel to prevent invaders getting aboard, set sentries and wait. They might try and contact us.'

I watched the sad lines of sailors being led off the beach towards the castle, and our crew rigging nets along the rails. I then scanned the horizon to see if there were any signs of rescue ships.

'Nothing to be seen, Princess,' said Alazne, looking over my shoulder.

'No, only fishing boats. It is well that there are no war vessels in the harbour, else we might be in more bother,' I replied.

'I believe that we are about to have visitors.' Alazne pointed out a small galley that had just appeared at the mouth of the harbour.

'Master!' several voices called out.

'Weapons ready; load the arbalests!' called William.

With great speed, the crew opened chests containing swords and crossbows and were soon standing against the rails.

The small galley approached us, steered by a tall, bearded man. 'Hello, state your business!' he shouted up at us.

William, not to be outdone in rudeness, shouted back, 'Crusaders, on the business of King Richard of England and Pope Innocent! Who are you?'

Silence greeted William's response, and we could see the man and his crew discussing matters.

'They must know who we are,' said Joan angrily, 'if they have taken crews from the other ships.'

'Aye, Your Highness, they know. I believe he intends to take queens and princesses as hostages.' He eyed us up and down. 'A pretty price Richard will have to pay to reclaim you two, I'll warrant.'

'I am not for sale,' I declared. 'Send him away.'

William laughed. 'Hostage-takers do not usually obey the demands of their victims. However, I'll try it.' He went to the rail to hail the boat, but the bearded man spoke first.

'You should land here. You will be taken care of until your ships are repaired.'

'My ship is fine,' said William. 'We'll have some water, though, if you can supply it at a fair price.'

'The other ships need repair. You can wait ashore until they are ready. My lord will be insulted if you do not accept his hospitality.'

'My lord has an army.'

More muttering ensued among the Griffons, until another offer came. 'Who are those women at the rail? Are you carrying doxies? We'll pay a fair price ... or their weight in water.' He sniggered and his scruffy-looking crew joined in.

'These are ladies of the court. One of them is my wife, and the others my daughters,' William lied. 'Apologise!'

'Really? Then they will be welcomed as *ladies* of Isaac's court and find some good positions there.' The Griffons curled up with laughter.

'We'll be back tomorrow. Your water butts will soon dry up, and Isaac's court will be all the merrier for some new *ladies*.' With that, the bearded man and his crew rowed off towards the beach near Lemesós Castle.

'Which one of us are you married to, William?' asked Queen Joan.

He laughed. 'Oh, any one of you would suit me.'

Amazed at his cheek, we all joined in with his laughter.

'I might not be your husband or papa, but it is my duty to keep you safe as if you were my own. Now then, we'll tighten up these boarding nets and I will set sentries tonight. Tomorrow, I will row around these few vessels we have and organise a proper defence ... including the sharing of water. I'm sure that Richard's fleet is heading our way. Cyprus is the last place the fleet could rendezvous before setting off on the final leg to Akko. He and his fleet commanders should be capable of working this conundrum out. It is surely only a matter of time.'

'Why do we not sail back west? We may encounter him earlier,' said Joan.

'It will only add more uncertainties to the equation, Your Highness. We are as likely to sail past them in the dark as run into them in the vastness of the ocean. My instinct is to hold on and let them come to us; it is the better option.'

Now that the sea was calm and the *Dione* steady, we brought out our bedding and clothes to dry in the sunshine. Alazne borrowed a knife from a seaman, then set to work cutting off the bottoms of her riding breeches. She then went below and returned wearing these cut-offs, her legs bare below the knee.

'There, Princess, is this not the best wear for living on a ship?' she said, parading before me.

'My word, Alazne,' said Joan, 'you do have trim legs. Is that comfortable?'

'Very easy to wear, Your Highness; it is a great freedom. Perhaps you could try it?'

'Yes, with your hair tied up you might pass for seamen at a distance,' said William. 'It might diminish the Griffons' interest in you.'

'Let's do it,' said Arrosa. 'I hated the way they stared at me so.'

'As did I, my sweet,' added Javier. 'I hate to contemplate your fate if they get their hands on you.'

'How many days shall we give Richard, William?' I asked.

'Three, Your Highness. Then we will set off back towards the previous rendezvous of Crete. The one we flew by in the storm ... if you agree?'

'Do we have enough water, master?' asked Joan.

'No, we will need to ration our reserve and perhaps obtain a little from the other ships; they have no passengers to cater for. I could put ashore at some other point on this island; there are rivers running into the sea, as I see from my chart.'

'Very well, that'll be our plan,' I agreed.

The Griffons returned every morning, once emptying a barrel of water into the sea. After this display of rudeness, they brought their boat nearer to make an offer for us women.

'Can you spear that barrel?' William asked one of his men, who was famed for his prowess with the crossbow.

'Aye, master, it is only fifty paces. I can get anything else in that vessel, including the sides.'

'There's an idea,' said William. 'Stick a bolt in the barrel and then make a start on the hull.'

'My pleasure, master. I've heard enough of their insults.'

The man wound up his arbalest and aimed through the side netting. When he released the trigger, the bolt flashed through the air and thumped into the emptied water barrel.

There was a shout of anger, and the Griffons waved their fists at us as a cheer rang across the water from our other ships at anchor nearby.

'Is that what you mean, Master William?' asked the happy arbalester as he reloaded his weapon.

'Exactly. Right in the barrel.'

The second bolt went a bit low, flying between the heads of two of its oarsmen, causing everyone in the boat to duck.

'Oh dear. Try again, lad.'

By the time the arbalester had reloaded, the oarsmen had recovered and were bending their backs furiously to propel the boats back to the shore. The next bolt walloped into the stern transom, and the third fell into the sea.

'That'll brighten up their day,' laughed William.

'How many crossbows can you muster?' asked Joan.

'Twelve,' William replied.

'You think that they might attack us at anchor?' I asked.

'I can't see any war galleys nearby, but they might have them elsewhere on the island. We are still in some danger.'

'How long will it take to put out to sea, master?' asked Joan.

'Not long, Your Highness. I'll leave the sail hoisted and un-reefed for a quick getaway, and we can cut through the anchor rope if needed; it depends more on the direction of the wind.'

'Let us pray that Richard is on his way.'

We slept fully clothed that night, ready to dash out on deck if the alarm was raised. I and the other women were now all wearing cut-offs for ease of movement.

In the morning, we piled out onto the open deck to find it busy. William saw us and called us over.

'Queens, princesses, ladies of the court.' He swept an arm down and across his knees in a passable imitation of a courtly bow. 'We went over to another ship and collected two barrels of water during the night; it's not much, but it improves our position.'

Stephen emerged from his station. Located near the front of the ship, it was no more than an oven in a shelter, set on stones laid on the deck and with an overhead canvas cover. He was only allowed to have a fire when the master deemed it safe, so a lot of the time he produced cold food from deep in the hold of the ship. Today, he had extracted a few chickens from a coop on deck, and so we were in for a treat; freshly cooked meat, bread and wine.

We settled down in front of the cabin steps and reached out eagerly for our rations.

'Have as much wine as you want,' said Stephen. 'It is water that is rationed.'

'What do we wash with?' asked Arrosa.

'Seawater, if you must,' he replied.

We wittered away all morning, moving into the shadow of the idle sail when the sun moved, and then into the dim cabin when it became too hot on deck. The wine and the worry were enough for me, and I fell asleep on my berth as the heat built during the afternoon.

The air was still oppressive when Alazne stirred above and woke me.

'There are noises on deck, Princess. Should we go and see?'

'It might be cooler out there. Let's go.'

There was snoring coming from Joan's side, so we left the queen and her ladies.

William greeted us. 'See there, Your Highness? There's some action.'

He pointed along the coast to the east. The sun had nearly touched the horizon in the west, but its light was enough to show some flashes near a headland some miles away.

'What's that?' I asked.

'That, Princess, is the flash of the sun on oars; there's a galley, possibly more than one, on its way. It seems that Isaac is going to reinforce his garrison in Lemesós; they have probably rowed around the island from Kyrenia. Richard will be opposed if he decides to land.'

'Alazne, go and get Queen Joan up here now. She needs to see this.'

I looked at William. 'Now what?'

'Now, Your Highness, do you feel any wind?'

'We're staying put?' I asked with dread in my stomach.

'I'll double the watch tonight. Pray that Richard turns up tomorrow.'

Joan arrived, and we were explaining the situation to her when a call from the sentry in the masthead confirmed our worst fears.

'Five galleys, master. Five in sight.'

'We're in trouble, Joan' I said. 'We should think about leaving this place tomorrow, if it's not too late.'

'Or if the wind gets up during the night,' added William.

We watched as the galleys sped along the coast towards us. When they were nearer, another hail came from the mast.

'War galleys, master.'

I felt sick. Danger was heading towards us and we had no means of escape. What would our fate be if they took the ship?

'Do you think that we should be properly dressed?' I asked Joan. 'They might respect our status if we are boarded.'

'You might be right. Look at us now.'

I looked. We each wore knee-length breeches and borrowed men's shirts with no shoes. Our faces were sunburned and our hair was salt-encrusted.

'It's worth a try,' said William. 'It'll be straight into a soldier's bordello, the way you are now. Make yourselves worth a ransom.'

As if in answer to my prayers, the galleys suddenly headed to the shore and grounded while still two or three miles away. We could see figures jumping down onto the sands.

'They're going ashore for a briefing, I shouldn't wonder, Your Highness. We might be safe tonight, but in the morning there will be danger. Pray for wind, ladies. We need some wind to get out of here.'

The morning brought little wind, certainly not enough to outrun those galleys. All five had been slid back into the sea and were heading towards us.

The closer they came, the more fearsome an aspect they presented; the oars flashed in the strengthening rays of the sun, and the water foamed.

I could hear a drum becoming louder and louder as the oars obeyed its beat. The mast was bereft of canvas, and the whole thing leaped forward through the sole power of the men on the benches.

Master William had his few crossbowmen ready against the rail, waiting for the order to loose. At the very last moment, I watched as the nearest steersmen, straining at their oars, turned the vessels aside and headed towards the harbour, one behind the other — seamanship at its most frightening.

'Clever rogues, I thought that we were going to be boarded!' William exclaimed.

I kept watching as the galleys slipped into harbour, their hulls hidden from view by the harbour walls. Next the crews appeared on the walls and lined up — soldiers, armoured and ready for war. Their commanders shouted orders and soon had them marching off towards Lemesós Castle.

'Your Highnesses, ladies and you scruffy crewmen of mine, you have been saved for another day. We could not have prevented that lot from boarding, and it would have gone badly for you women,' said William. 'They must be hatching some plan ashore, or perhaps they do not have the authority to attack; we shall see. But you should pray that King Richard is not far off.'

'I'm keeping a knife hidden in my gown,' Alazne spat. 'If there's any likelihood of being debauched, someone will lose their balls before I surrender.'

The next morning, we arrived on the afterdeck to find Master William hanging over the rail, arguing with someone.

'Your Highnesses, ladies and Captain Javier, come and see this,' he said.

We lined up against the rail and looked down into the two vessels riding below. They were four-oared boats, with the spaces between the rowers filled with boxes and barrels.

'What's this, Master William?' I ventured.

'A bribe, Princess, to get us off this ship,' he replied.

'What's the offer?'

'Bread, fresh meats, wine, and fruits. More of the same if we go ashore. And they're suspiciously friendly.'

'I'll talk to them,' said Joan. Her ladies had dressed her in shimmering green silk, and her long blonde hair flowed free above her shoulders. She was already the tallest among we women, but court shoes enhanced her height even further. I wondered if it was wise to place such a temptation before the false Griffons. 'Who are you?' she asked, poking her head out over the rail.

The fellow in command of the boat replied coarsely, 'Dimitriou. Who are you — Aphrodite?' This remark caused much merriment among his half-naked oarsmen.

'I am Joan, Queen of Sicily and sister of Richard Coeur de Lion of England, and I am a pilgrim on my way to the Holy Shrines of Jerusalem, under the protection of Mother Church. I expect that you respect my position, being a good Christian.' She was at her most imperious, not at all what we were used to.

There was silence below, broken only by the lapping of the water against the sides of the boats.

'You have supplies, I believe, fellow,' the haughty Joan continued.

'Indeed, Your Highness, sent by our master, Isaac, Emperor of Cyprus.'

'Then send them up. And convey to your master our profound thanks.'

Joan looked at William and whispered, 'Get lines down and collect what they have to offer before they change their mind.'

The offerings were quickly pulled aboard.

The man below made another offer. 'If it pleases Your Highness, I have instructions to offer you my lord's invitation to avail yourself of his hospitality at his castle in Lemesós.' He had his cap off his head by now and was attempting to make a bow in the rocking boat.

'Thank you, we'll give the matter some consideration,' Joan replied, whereupon she withdrew her head from his view and left the seamen to get on with it. Emperor Isaac's envoy was soon exhorting his crew to make haste back to shore, no doubt to report his conversation.

'Oh, Joan, you were marvellous,' I said joyfully, planting a kiss on her cheek. 'You took those supplies right out of his hands.'

'Our humble thanks to you, Your Highness,' added William. 'Should we open the containers and see what you have gained for us?'

'Please do, Master William. I'm going to sit in the shade and cool down, if you please.'

We sampled some of Emperor Isaac's offerings later that day.

'This is delicious,' exclaimed Alazne, her chin dripping with red Cyprus wine.

'This lamb suits me,' I said, biting into the freshly cooked meat, 'but what do we do if Richard doesn't turn up? Isaac knows who we are now, Joan.'

'True, but think on; we are valuable as hostages, so we shouldn't be slung into the stews.'

'That will depend on how Isaac views things,' Alazne said.

It was then that our miracle occurred.

'Sails, sails in sight! To the south-west — galleys!' called the lookout from the top of the mast.

Master William dashed up to the afterdeck to see for himself. We followed and crowded against the rail.

'Richard!' cried Joan. 'It must be Richard. Oh Lord, we give thee thanks, our prayers are fulfilled.'

Soon we could see the men on the deck of the first galley — the other sails that had been spotted were still many miles away on the horizon. The standards flying at the prow and stern quickly became visible.

'The king!' cried Joan. 'Richard's banner and the three lions of England.'

We pressed against the rail, and the figure standing out from the crowded afterdeck gave a wave and removed his helm. Even at a distance, His Highness shone.

I counted eighteen oars. Thirty-six rowers stilled on a command, and the great war vessel slowed as it passed us to gain entry into the harbour of Lemesós.

Soon a six-oared boat came back out of the harbour and made its way towards us.

'That's known as a *snekkja*, a Norse vessel,' said William. It was now the transport of King Richard, and the lions of England flew at its stern.

It slid alongside us. Our anti-boarding nets had been removed, so the king could vault across without waiting for the security of mooring ropes. He dashed across the deck and up the steps to embrace both Joan and myself.

'Sister, Berengaria, thank the Lord that you are safe. No matter what the Church says on the issue, we will not be separated again, else this Crusade will end before we set foot on holy soil. Where's the master? William, my eternal thanks.'

'Oh, Richard, do not upset yourself so,' said Joan calmly. 'We have had quite an adventure, your betrothed and I.'

'Indeed, my betrothed.' He turned to me. 'I will say this, and all who hear it shall take note. I have loved this lady since we were youths, and her beauty and her wit are plain for all to see. But now she has also demonstrated courage —' he paused and beckoned forward our ladies — 'as have all the ladies present. I salute you, ladies, warriors all. Now, tell me why you are not safely within the harbour walls.'

'We'll let Master William tell the tale, Richard,' I said, with my arms around his waist.

William's explanation did not take long, and before he had finished, Richard's face had turned red and his eyes flashed.

'No, no, enough!' he roared. 'I'm going to sort this out. First I'm going to extract my galleys from the port — they are in danger trapped within. Then I'll get my fleet commanders together and we'll hatch a plan for the destruction of this false emperor. And we'll send some soldiers ashore to find the crews who were abducted from those beached cogs over there.'

He planted a kiss on my lips, but before I could react he was over the side and in his *snekkja*, heading back to the harbour.

'Make the most of that,' said Joan. 'He's not one to dwell on romance or emotion.'

'So I see,' I replied. I caught Alazne's eye, and she managed a weak smile of encouragement. 'What will we do now, William?'

'We shall watch the comings and goings, Your Highness. I suspect there will be a lot of those. Look yonder, the rest of the fleet is almost upon us; this anchorage will soon be full.'

'See there,' said Joan, excited, 'Richard's galleys are leaving the harbour. He has them safely out of the clutches of our unseen tormentor.'

The tableau unfolded before us. Richard's galleys came to anchor nearby as his *snekkja* sped towards them so he could talk to the crew. More kept coming over the horizon.

'Now the port is denied us,' observed William. 'The Griffons are stretching a boom across the entrance.'

'What's a boom?' asked Arrosa, still clinging to Javier.

'A floating barrier.'

'Oh, well, they'll need to land on the beach, then. They cannot block all of that,' said Joan.

CHAPTER TWELVE

We were blessed with calm weather that afternoon and evening, but the king did not come to visit. Still, there was much to see as the fleet prepared for action. What Richard had in mind we did not know, until a *snekkja* came alongside with a messenger aboard.

'The king sends news for Queen Joan and Princess Berengaria. If I may come aboard?'

'Come on up,' invited Master William, who then instructed Jacob to search the man for weapons. 'Can't take any chances, Your Highnesses. There are boats flitting all around us now; he could be from anywhere.'

'What is it you have to say, fellow?' I asked.

'The king is going ashore to see if he can speak to Isaac of Cyprus. He says that you will serve him best by remaining here until the matter is resolved, Your Highness. The *snekkjas* are moving soldiers and supplies around the fleet so that if it comes to war, we can assault the beach in the right order. Those cogs over there are the type known as *hippagōga*. They have ramps built into their sides and can be grounded on the beach to unload their cargo of horses. The king's horse will be among the first to land.'

'But first he will try diplomacy?' I asked.

'Indeed, Your Highness, that is his wish. Our target is Jerusalem, not Lemesós.'

'Very well,' said Joan. 'Send him our love, and tell him that our prayers are with him.'

'Your Highness, I will straightaway inform His Highness of your love and prayers.'

The messenger climbed back down into his craft and was soon speeding across the water to where Richard's galley lay at anchor. Joan was standing near me and shuffled about, clearly uneasy.

'Don't worry, Joan, the king is in command of this. Whoever this Isaac is, he should tremble.'

She faced me with a look of concern. 'May I talk with you privately, Berengaria? Something bothers me, and it is not Richard at war.'

'Oh,' I replied, 'Alazne, could you leave us please?'

'Princess,' she murmured and went to join Arrosa and Javier down on the working deck.

Joan and I were alone on the afterdeck, save for William, who effected to be watching the activities of the fleet.

'He will win this skirmish, Berengaria, of that I have no doubt. The sea contains more men and weapons of war than Isaac could ever muster on his little island. But I wish to speak to you about love, if you would permit?'

'There is no subject from which I would shy away, Joan,' I replied.

We paused as we watched the king's *snekkja* leave his galley and head for the shore.

'He is not on it,' Joan decided. 'I recognise those two figures in the stern; they are ambassadors of old. He is testing Isaac. Look, the beach has been made secure.'

On the beach, a small party of warriors had already landed. As we watched, they formed a protective cordon for Richard's embassy. They were observed by a crowd of Griffons, but no aggression was offered, and eventually the ambassadors landed. After some discussion, they were provided with steeds and escorted towards the castle.

Joan spoke again. 'Some might not notice, but my lady Pavot has become very close to your Alazne. Pavot has some history with other women, too.'

'Is that all you are worried about?'

'No, at present it is only obvious to me. But Richard also has an uncertain history in that regard. The season of Lent is now behind us, and I can't see you leaving Cyprus unwed.' Joan took my hand in hers. 'There are rumours about my brother, Berengaria. He has sired a brat, I know that, but his relationship with Philip of France has also come into question.'

'Really? But they have just quarrelled, have they not?'

'Over Alys, but that is a matter which even friends might argue over.'

'Ah, I thought that your mother was holding something back.'

'She moves people like chess pieces, Berengaria. She wished to see you married before the rumours reached you.'

'There seems to be one way to determine the issue,' I offered. 'Richard has asked me to marry him, and I shall do so.'

'You have much courage, Berengaria. God bless you.' Joan paused. 'When Richard wins the skirmish here, he will invest Cyprus and control the land. It will require some adjustments to deal with the change in leadership — a new overlord, for instance. We may be here for a longer period than we once thought necessary. Therefore, I'm sure that Richard will decide to marry you here, before we set off to Akko.'

It was late in the day when Richard's ambassadors returned, and their *snekkja* was barely visible in the gloom when it passed us on its way back to Richard's ship. I was with Alazne, gnawing on a chicken bone, when we spied it.

'What did Queen Joan say to you in such secrecy earlier?' Alazne asked.

I looked around to see if anyone was near. We moved over to the side of the ship furthest from the busy waterway. 'Joan has noticed you and Pavot.'

'Oh! Are we to part? I'll die.'

'No, my sweet, but you should be cautious. Maintain a distance in public and be careful in private. But Joan said something more immediate: she pointed out that if Richard decides to occupy Cyprus, he might well begin his rule with a wedding here in Lemesós.'

This revelation was greeted with silence, which was broken when Arrosa and Javier approached from behind and asked what we were discussing. I explained, and Arrosa was more excited about the prospect of an island wedding than Alazne.

When I awoke the next morning, Joan and her ladies had already gone up on deck.

'Come on, Princess, let's not miss anything,' said Alazne.

'What are we wearing today?' I asked.

'Better make it gowns — the king might visit.'

'Oh, the king! Where's my gown from yesterday?'

'On the deck. It will be all right, nobody's stood on it.'

Alazne retrieved the gown and helped me dress, and we made our way up together.

It was scarcely light, yet there was movement everywhere. Boats scudded about, and I could hear the whinnying of horses.

'Master William, good morning,' I greeted. 'What do you know?'

'Your Highness, you're in time to witness the seaborne invasion of an island. We've had no direct word from the king, but everything points to a landing. I've dropped a stern anchor to keep the *Dione* steady and the steerboard side of her facing the beach. We should have a good view of today's events. There'll be food brought to you in a while, and in the meantime here's some of that excellent Cypriot wine, if you please.'

I drank and felt warmer for it in the chilly mists drifting across the surface of the water. Then Javier turned up with Arrosa in tow.

'The king did not receive the answer he wanted then, William?' said Javier.

'Seems not. Isaac is likely to regret turning away the King of England.'

'Are they going to fight, my love?' asked Arrosa.

'It seems so. I've never seen a waterborne invasion, but I understand from the success of William the Conqueror that the Normans have a certain skill in the matter.'

'A little wine, Captain?' offered William.

'Thank you, master. An excellent way to start the day: Cypriot wine and a battle. There has been naught but excitement along the way. Princess Berengaria, thank you for choosing me.'

'I'm glad that you feel that way, Captain, but my betrothed is about to launch himself at a hostile shore. A short prayer might be prudent.'

'We'll join you, Berengaria,' said Joan. 'William, do you have your Bible? Let's hear from you.'

William dived into a hatch at the stern and reappeared with his well-thumbed Bible. 'Something for the day from the Ephesians,' he said. 'It seems suitable.' He began reading loudly. By the time he reached the end of his chosen passage, he was at such a pitch they must have heard his exhortations throughout the fleet. He stood for a moment, head bowed, before stating, 'There, that's all I have time for. Carry on yourselves, if you wish. I have things to see to.' He gave Joan the Bible before dashing down onto the working deck.

I pointed at the lines of soldiers forming up along the beach. 'It seems that Isaac is about to set his play in motion.' My stomach churned; how could men in boats possibly attack a beach filled with steady troops defending their territory?

It was full daylight now, and we could see that some of Richard's fleet had been moved around during the night. Just out of bolt range were three of the middling galleys, which were full of archers.

'English archers!' cried Javier. 'By the devil's horns, Richard has English archers!'

Behind the archers were half a dozen *snekkjas* filled with men-at-arms, and lastly two of the horse-carrying *hippagóga*.

'This should be enlightening,' said Javier, taking a soldier's interest in the array. 'If Isaac is not properly organised, he is about to receive a nasty surprise.'

In the centre of the fleet sat King Richard's galley, easily identified by the banners flying. Although it was two hundred paces away across the water from us, I could see his head, topped with a crown and shining in the morning sun. He was cloaked in red. Also in his vessel were men with flags, who seemed to be sending signals to those others lined up ready to attack the Griffons.

I felt quite ill now. This day was not going to end without bloodshed, and I prayed for Richard and his men. Alazne came and supported me with an arm around my waist. Then Joan, equally unhappy and seeing my distress, came to stand on my other side.

'They're going in,' said Javier.

A trumpet sounded and a flag waved from Richard's galley. The ships carrying the archers began to move towards the shore. They were met by the crews of the five galleys that we had watched coming down the coast earlier. They hurled stones from slings and bolts from crossbows; then the troops on land added their efforts so that our boats were met by more volleys of crossbow bolts, the first falling short and dropping into the sea, causing no damage. Richard's archers, together with the rowers, were prepared for this and had brought with them wicker pavises; the archers held them up to guard the rowers. Our men, when they came into range of the Griffons, were not harmed, save for a few bolts that found gaps.

When they were about one hundred paces from the beach, the pavises were set aside. Standing up in the boats, Richard's archers let fly.

The results were devastating. Isaac's troops, helpless on the sand, received volley after volley of arrow showers. Soon the strand was cleared of standing men, and those of the galleys' crews who were not struck down jumped overboard and swam for their lives. Isaac's men further up the beach ran off inland to seek the shelter of the trees.

This was when the second part of Richard's plan came into effect. With the archers' galleys remaining a little offshore to keep the Griffons at bay, the *snekkjas* carrying the men-at-arms came swiftly through and headed for the beach, as arrows continued to rain. Thus denying the Griffons any advancement, the infantry-carrying boats swept up onto the beach and disgorged their armoured threat. There being little resistance left to confront, they soon took up defensive positions at the treeline. Then, on another trumpet blast and flag signal, the horse transports began their dignified approach under sail. They reached the waterline, let down their ramps and freed the cavalry horses.

By this time I was feeling much better and asked Javier if he had finished the wine.

'That went well,' he laughed as he passed the flagon. 'I've never seen the like. Oh, look, there goes Richard.'

Richard's vessel was flying across the water, and it landed so far up the beach that the king stepped ashore with dry feet. A great cheer echoed from his ships, and soon he was atop his great charger, a magnificent beast all caparisoned in red and adorned with the three golden lions of England. After spending a few moments in conference with his captains, Richard gave a wave and set off with his army following.

'My God,' said William, now back on the afterdeck. 'It is not yet midday, and already he has Cyprus in his grasp.'

Our lookout gave a shout from the masthead. 'That big galley's moving, master!'

'So it is. He's heading for the harbour; I'll warrant that they're going to take that boom out.'

The giant warship was on the move, sixteen oars per side lifting and dipping to the beat of the drum. The water rose up before the cutting bow as it gained speed.

'They'll not keep that up for long,' said William. 'The pace is exhausting.'

When the galley neared the entrance to the harbour, the disbelieving sentries on the ends of the jetties began to shout and run off towards the shore end.

The galley's oars were lifted inboard and the rowers tucked in their heads, and it ran into the boom. Crates, logs, small boats and ropes were sent flying all over, some of them coming to rest on the ship itself. Nonetheless, it careered through, and the boom was destroyed.

The oars were seized once more, and the vessel was guided alongside the pier. The oarsmen came off it at speed; they were soldiers now, fully armed and armoured. Running along the pier, they despatched any Griffons too slow to disperse, and by this means took control of the harbour.

The seizure of Lemesós was complete, but where was the king?

'It is very quiet now,' said Alazne. 'I'd like to know what's going on ashore.'

'I have an idea that they'll be chasing Isaac back into the hills,' said William.

'What is the date?' asked Joan. 'I've quite lost track of time.'

'I keep a diary, Your Highness,' replied William. 'Today is the seventh day of May in the year of our Lord 1191.'

'Thank you. It is quite warm; I think that I might stay out a while. That cabin is oppressive in the heat. What do you think, Berengaria?'

'I favour it. Has Stephen anything special in mind for our evening meal, William? We might have won an island this day.'

'I'll send him ashore to see if there is any fresh meat to be had. And, as a special treat, we have some tables in the hold — we'll see about digging them out and have a meal up here on the afterdeck.'

'What about the sailors?' I asked. 'They deserve a celebration too.'

'I'll see to that. As long as I restrict the wine, they can feast on the main deck.'

By late afternoon, Stephen had returned in the ship's little rowing boat and seemed quite cheerful. He had taken with him two of the ugliest seamen, armed with wicked curved swords that they had picked up on their travels. Therefore, all three returned safely, laden with fresh comestibles.

'Come up,' hailed William, as Stephen climbed aboard. 'Now, tell us what you have discovered on the shore.'

'It was very exciting — there were lots of soldiers and sailors gathered round the castle,' said Stephen. 'There had been fighting nearby for a few days, as some of the sailors from those beached cogs had freed themselves and skirmished with the Griffons. King Richard visited the castle briefly and ordered some arrangements for Your Highnesses, and then he left to chase after Isaac, who has gone into the hills. The local shopkeepers were doing grand business with our troops, and some women have set up a tent for private business, begging your pardon, Your Highnesses. I found meats and other supplies, at some cost, Master William, and I added some of this local wine to my list.'

'What lodgings are there, Stephen?' asked Joan.

'There's a pavilion going up, and other marquees and tents. The castle is being prepared for the ladies, and there'll be a messenger coming out to see you in the morning, Your Highnesses.'

'Thank you,' said Joan, as Stephen bustled off to prepare the feast.

'Lodgings in a castle — that will be nice,' I said.

'A proper closet, too,' added Alazne.

'We'll have a bedchamber,' squealed Arrosa. 'Hear that, Javier?'

Her remark made me think of my forthcoming wedding night, and my stomach started to churn. I excused myself and dashed off to the privy closet.

I did not go back up to the feast on the afterdeck; I went to bed and lay thinking. After a while, Alazne came down to find me.

'What's wrong, Princess?' she whispered.

'Oh, Alazne, it's nothing. You go and enjoy the night; I shall be well in the morning.'

'If you're sure, Princess. I'll sleep on the spare berth tonight, if you wish — then I won't disturb you.'

I turned to see her better. 'You are thoughtful. Do you know how much I love you, Alazne?'

'Yes, Princess, I know. Now, try and sleep. It might be another busy day tomorrow.'

Joan woke me the next morning. 'Berengaria, there's news,' she said. 'We are going ashore.'

'What time is it, Joan?'

'Quite early. The sun is just up, but there are things going on, and Richard has asked us to go to the castle.'

'I suppose that means dressing up a bit,' I said, throwing back the covers.

'Oh, yes, I'll get some fresh water sent down.'

'I'll go and open your chest, Princess, and choose something for you to wear,' said Alazne.

I felt much better than I had the previous day. Most of my doubts had gone, and my confidence was renewed.

William had a canvas curtain rigged across the entry to our quarters to give us privacy while we washed and dressed. When we'd finished, our courtly appearance drew cheers from the appreciative crewmen. Joan asked for them to be gathered together so that she could address them.

'I want to thank you for your efforts to keep us and this ship, the *Dione*, safe through stormy times. It has been difficult and there have been deaths, but your courage and seamanship have seen us through. For that, I thank you. I do not know if we will be travelling further on this vessel, so we will say goodbye and wish you a safe return to your families.'

Her words received an appreciative response.

Now we were wearing gowns, it proved difficult to clamber over the side and into a *snekkja*. Our ladies were stuffed into the bows while Joan and I tried to keep out of the steersman's way at the stern as he pulled his oar this way and that. The harbour entrance was still awash with floating debris from the demolition of the boom, but we pushed through it and came to a rest against the pier. An armoured man pulled us up onto the boards and announced his intention of walking us the few paces from the harbour to the castle.

'Where is King Richard?' Joan asked. 'And who are you?'

'The king is chasing after Isaac Comnenus, Your Highness. I am scribe to His Highness, and my name is Hugo de Mara.'

'Thank you, Hugo. Let us inspect this castle of Lemesós.'

Various groups were at work; some were repairing weapons, and some fishermen were preparing to go to sea.

'We told them that they had an army to feed. If they want the business, they will be supplying us with fresh fish before long, I'll warrant.'

There were wagons trundling by, loaded with Griffon corpses. Then we passed a group of men — sailors, judging by their garb.

'These are our men. They were taken prisoner when their ships ran aground, but they freed themselves and attacked their guards. Well done, you men, well done!' Hugo called out to them.

'They seem quite merry, Hugo,' I observed.

'They have liberated the wine store in the castle, Your Highness; the cellarer was happy to unlock the door when they paid him a visit.'

We stopped in front of the castle.

'Is this a Byzantine construction?' I asked.

'Yes, just a tower. We would name it a donjon, with some wooden buildings set around it.'

We meandered round the various buildings; there were stables, the farrier's open-sided hut, the armourer's forge, and one other large hut. Over to one side, some men were erecting a gaudy pavilion.

'No motte, Hugo?'

'No, Your Highness; the ground is very hard. They build straight up; it is quite secure, and the guard chamber is difficult to reach up those steep steps.'

'There is a church somewhere?' I asked.

'Indeed, the chapel of Saint George, around the back.'

'Where are we staying?' asked Joan, not entirely content.

'There are three levels, Your Highness. The guard hall, then a floor given over to senior household knights and their families, and then the top floor, with the bedchambers where you will be lodged.'

'How many bedchambers does it have, Hugo?'

'Two separate quarters with two bedchambers each, and a common chamber to share.'

'You say that there are quarters for married knights, Hugo?' asked Javier.

'Indeed, do you fit into that category?'

'Yes. Meet my wife, Arrosa, tending lady to Princess Berengaria.'

'Then I shall allocate you a chamber.'

The steps up to the entrance were extremely steep; the narrow treads made it difficult to run up them and easier to defend. The entrance was a tunnel with arrow slits in the walls. This brought us into the guard hall, where some garrison soldiers lived.

'Those stairs lead down to the great hall in the undercroft,' explained Hugo, 'and this one,' he added, leading the way, 'is to the upper chambers.'

Arrosa galloped up behind me, and when we reached the next level, she and Javier took one of the chambers set aside for knights.

When we reached the next floor, Hugo said, 'The chambers to the left and right are for your use, Your Highnesses. They are similar, and the further doors are where your tending ladies can be accommodated, if they choose. We eat in the grand hall in the undercroft later tonight. When the king returns, he will entertain everyone in the pavilion presently being erected outside. If Your Highnesses would like to inspect the chambers?'

I walked through the wooden door held open by Hugo to find a richly furnished chamber with a large bed taking up half of the space.

'Oh, joy,' I whispered.

There were similar exclamations coming from across the corridor from Joan, Pavot, and Torène.

Hugo watched as I tested the straw-filled bed. 'Does that please you, Your Highness?' he asked politely.

'Indeed, it is more than we have had for many a month,' I answered.

'And there is more, Your Highness. Beyond that curtain,' he said, pointing to one corner of the chamber, 'is a small chamber with a truckle bed for your tending lady, or she may use one of the other chambers. And behind the curtain in the opposite corner is a chamber for washing. We can provide water for your use, and there is a bathhouse, a Byzantine pleasure, a few paces from the castle. Just inform the attendant, and he will escort you there. The place will be closed to all except you.'

'Attendant?' I asked.

'At all times there will be two armed sentries at the bottom of the stairs and a personal attendant at the top. You may if you wish ask for a woman to assist, but the man is trustworthy and capable of carrying heavy things on your behalf, and he has no interest in women.'

'Oh!' I believed that he meant that the attendant was a eunuch. 'You've thought of everything, Hugo, thank you. Now, will you send someone to inform the king that his betrothed and his sister are waiting for him to greet them?'

'I can, of course, Your Highness, but … he might not like being summoned.'

Joan appeared in the doorway. 'Then don't summon him. Invite him.'

Hugo gave an uncertain bow and made to leave the chamber. 'As Your Highness wishes.'

'Good,' exclaimed Joan, 'and may God smile upon you.'

'You are wicked, Joan,' I said when he had gone. 'He is in for a difficult time.'

'*We* have had a difficult time getting here. How do you like that bed? It's enormous.'

I had a thought. 'Alazne, go and tell that attendant that we want our chests off the sea and in the castle. I intend to test the Byzantine bath hall and dress appropriately for this evening's meal.'

'What a splendid thought, Berengaria,' said Joan. 'Include me, Pavot, and Torène in that, Alazne.'

'And collect Arrosa as you go, Alazne, before she gets entangled in her bridal bedchamber,' I added.

We all had a titter at that.

When Alazne had gone, Joan put an arm around my shoulders. 'I'll be here to support you, Berengaria, if you ever want to discuss things,' she murmured.

'Thank you, Joan,' I replied. 'I am settled on this course; it is what should happen.'

'I know, but you might be a little divided in your emotions.'

'I am, but I have discussed it with Alazne, and I am determined to find my way through.'

A short while later we heard laughter rising up the stairs, and then our ladies burst in.

'Princess! Oh, you should see the baths; they are all marble —' began Alazne.

'And hot and cold water —' added Arrosa.

'And there are female and male attendants,' said Pavot.

'And public privies,' said Torène with a frown.

'What do you mean, public privies?' asked Joan.

'Well,' said Pavot, 'there's a chamber, and it has marble benches with holes set against the walls —'

'And a trench with a stream of running water beneath,' interrupted Alazne.

'You sit over a hole along the walls, in full view of everyone else,' said Torène. 'When you're finished, women come around with buckets and sponges and there's another hole on the front of the bench, where they push wet sponges through and —'

'Clean you off,' finished Alazne.

'And where are these male attendants?' asked Joan.

'When you go into the inner baths, you lie on a marble slab, where they massage you with oils and unguents. You can choose a masseur, male or female.'

'We can go as soon as you like, Princess,' replied Alazne. 'We will don loose robes and cross over to the bath hall. When we are ready, we can come back dressed for Hugo's feast. The clothes chests are on the way — I will set out our gowns and they will be taken across for us. We can dress over there.'

I kissed her on the forehead and thanked her for her efforts.

We all undressed and put on thin white robes and sandals. We then made our way down the castle steps and across the dusty path, which led us to the ancient bathhouse.

The entrance hall was built from black marble, with small windows set high in the walls, and it was lit by flaming torches in sconces. We were guided to sit in chairs, then six young women entered. They were clad only in epitogas.

'Your Highnesses, we are your hostesses this evening,' uttered the leading woman in a voice so deep and smooth that it left no echo. 'We will conduct you to the *laconicum*.'

One by one, the women took each of us by the hand and guided us into the first chamber — a steam-filled circle so thickly misted that I could hardly see across it.

'We will remain here until the pores of your skin have opened, and the cleansing process can begin,' the lead hostess explained through the mist.

'Alazne, where are you?' I called.

'Lost in the mist, Princess.'

'You sound as if you are on the opposite wall.'

'I'll feel my way around.'

She and her guardian soon settled next to me and my young hostess.

'I've never been this hot, Princess,' gasped Alazne.

'Nor I,' I replied.

Our hostesses turned away and softly conversed with each other in their own tongue.

'I'll have to go,' Joan called. 'I'm sliding off this marble bench.'

'Your Highness,' said a voice, 'we will not cause you distress. Come with me.'

I heard the rustle of cloth as my hostess grasped my hand and led me through the steam.

We emerged into a cooler and clearer chamber, which was mostly taken up by a deep pool.

'*Frigus piscinam*,' explained the voice. 'You may retain your garments or remove them as you wish.'

Alazne dropped her wrap and jumped into the water. She screeched as she surfaced. 'Mother of God! It's freezing in here.'

I jumped in after her and gasped as I surfaced. The others were still lined up, making up their minds. Then Joan threw down her wrap and joined us, and Pavot pushed Torène in before jumping in herself. Arrosa soon followed.

One of the hostesses threw some floating rings into the pool and we enjoyed a game of throwing and catching. I had not felt so light-hearted for many a month and was reluctant to leave when the lead hostess announced that it was time to go.

'Where are we going now?' asked Joan. As we climbed out of the pool, we were immediately wrapped in hot towels and dressed in silk nether breeches.

'You may wear a loose linen branc to cover your front, if you wish,' said the lead hostess. 'Next we will visit the *suspendisse locus*, where you will meet your *masculum agilem*. If you prefer, you may have a *feminam agilem*.'

I heard the sweet music of a lute before we entered the chamber. It was another marble hall with several marble tables, each with an almost naked man standing next to it. They had black beards and resembled the statues of the Roman gods I had seen in Italy, with gleaming, muscled torsos. The lute was accompanied by the sound of running water, and the air was filled with sweet fragrances.

'Lie face down on a table of your choice,' instructed the lead hostess. 'The massage will begin when you are ready.'

I let Joan step forward and watched as her man greeted her in gentle tones, and then I chose the table next to her. Alazne followed and settled on the one behind me.

My man helped me to settle and threw a bucket of warm, soapy water over my back. He then produced a giant sea sponge and proceeded to scrub me down from neck to buttocks, and then from the top of my thighs down to my feet. I lay with my head on my arms and relaxed.

'Turn, please,' he said, and my hostess covered my chest and hips with small towels and helped me onto my back. This was followed by another bucket of warm water, then he began to work his way around my body from the front.

'The men will wrap you in sheets and when you have dried off, the women will begin the massage with precious oils and unguents,' said the lead hostess.

The oiling was much more intimate than the douching, but the women's hands were warm and gentle. They searched out every ache and teased it away.

'Now you will be wrapped in sheets and taken into the final chamber, where young women will help you with your face and hair,' said the lead hostess. 'Please take your time. Your clothes will be waiting for you when you are finished.'

I sat up and gazed around the chamber. Everyone had a dreamy expression on their faces, though our hair lay flat.

'Our ladies know much about hair and how it can be fashioned, Your Highness,' the lead hostess quickly assured me. 'Please tell them how you like it, and they will comply with your wishes.'

For the next treatment we were led to padded chairs, where more young women gave us facial rubs and soaped our hair, rinsing it with spring water. It was then mostly dried off with towels, after which the women stood and waved fans at our heads.

CHAPTER THIRTEEN

It was dark when we left the bathhouse, and the way was lit by braziers. Now we were fully dressed as court ladies and preceded by an armed guard as we moved towards the steps of the castle. Hugo was waiting at the foot.

'Your Highnesses, let me welcome you back. Did you enjoy your visit to the baths?' he asked.

'It was superb, Hugo, superb. Thank you for arranging it,' said Joan. 'Did you find the king?'

'Yes, Your Highness, although he was not pleased to see me. He named me for a finicky clerk.'

'You informed him that we are here?'

'Indeed. He said that he would return on the morrow. I thought him in a foul mood because he had lost the emperor; Isaac has escaped to Nikosia. It is a walled city, which will make it difficult to winkle him out. Now, if you will allow, I'll take you to the great hall, where we can feed you properly. I understand that the food supply on a ship is somewhat limited.'

We climbed the stairs to the guard floor and, confusingly, the steps to the great hall led downwards.

Hugo explained this as we descended. 'Outside we climbed up to the guard floor level. The great hall is underneath the guard, and so we go down again. This is Byzantine architecture, thus the entrance to the castle is guarded, and the hall is kept secure. There are no windows and the base of the castle wall is three paces thick. Ah, here we are. Please to be seated, Your Highnesses.'

The hall had a single table set out in the centre, with buffet tables along one wall. Some of the food was steaming hot, and there were plenty of greens and fruit. I made selection and chose a chair in the centre of the table. Joan sat next to me while Hugo stood proudly at one end, watching. There was some urgent whispering behind me, and I turned to see Alazne and Arrosa in discussion with Pavot and Torène.

'What ails thee, Pavot?' asked Joan.

'Where to sit, Your Highness,' she answered.

Joan looked at me and I nodded to the chairs opposite.

'At the table, where else?'

Hugo's eyebrows lifted a little, but he smiled and held back chairs for our ladies to sit. There were only two goblets on the table, but Joan wafted a hand and soon we all had a drink.

'We have suffered together, we have laughed and cried together, and this day we have bathed together, so why should we not eat together?' said Joan. 'To your health, ladies, and more adventuring.'

'Hugo, sit and join us,' I said. 'We will hear from you about the king's war. Call for a goblet; this is fine wine.'

'Thank you, Your Highness,' he said. 'You are very kind.' He chose the chair at one end of the table, careful not to pull it too near. When his glass was full and he had offered us a libation, he began. 'King Richard set out with his army early yesterday, and they discovered the Griffons in a valley not far off. The king took up a position on a hill, and the Griffons ran out of the valley and occupied the hill opposite. There were many insults, and just as many slingshots and bolts hurled cross the space between the hills, but little damage was done. They had twice as many men in the field as the king, so it was as well the armies did not engage.' He took a drink from his goblet. 'We found this wine when we seized the castle. It's local from special grapes — quite good don't you think, Your Highnesses?'

'Very,' agreed Joan, joining him in a long draught. 'So the day did not end in a stalemate, I suspect.'

'Correct, Your Highness. The king grew bored, spurred his horse and galloped down the hill, across the valley and charged straight at the Griffons' position.'

'What next?' I demanded.

'The rest of our army galloped after him, of course. He scattered the Griffons and most of them ran off, but before his knights caught up with him, Richard spied Isaac and went thundering at him, knocking him off his horse. Those of Isaac's supporters who were left standing surrounded him, which allowed him time to remount and flee.'

Joan quickly emptied her glass and held it up for a refill, which came with equal swiftness. 'God Bless King Richard, the victor,' she proclaimed.

We all cheered.

The night descended into revelry, and someone got up a tabor. Hugo was a good raconteur, and he kept us amused with tales of soldiers and their adventures.

Waking, I found two arms across my body. I manged to get upright. The arms belonged to Alazne and Joan. All of us were fully gowned, although without shoes. I shuffled off the end of the bed and made my way to the privy closet.

'Good morning,' said Joan. 'I can't hear anything outside — is it time for Prime? Where are Pavot and Torène? Ugh! My mouth.'

'Fear not, Your Highness,' I heard Pavot reply. 'We are here.'

I emerged from the closet and grabbed the water carafe and goblet from the sideboard. 'Will we see Richard today, Joan?'

'Who knows? We are not his highest priority. Killing Griffons seems to have become something of an obsession since he landed here.'

There was a call from the stair head. 'Your Highnesses?' It was Hugo. 'May I approach?'

'Come in,' I answered. 'Everybody else in is here; we'll find room for you.'

He entered, casting his eyes at the ceiling, just in case he caught a glimpse of something he shouldn't. 'It will be a busy day, Your Highness. Preparations for the return of the king are almost complete.'

'Complete!' remarked Joan. 'They did not seem so last night.'

'You noticed little on the way up from the hall, Your Highness,' Pavot informed her.

Arrosa laughed. 'Javier says that I'm not to drink wine anymore. He says I fell asleep on him,' she said.

Hugo coughed, perhaps unused to such frank discussions in a bedchamber full of women.

'Worry not, Hugo. Just tell us what part we are to play,' I said, smiling.

'Thank you, Your Highness. There are a few things that you can note. Firstly, I have tried to keep activities on the roof to a minimum, but I will send sentries up this morning to keep a lookout for the king. You may hear their footsteps above your heads.'

'Have they not been up there these past few days, Hugo?' asked Joan.

'No, Your Highness. With the king and his army in the field, there was no need, and he has nearly all the soldiers with him. I have only a few left to guard this place.'

'Without asking for a miracle, when do you expect King Richard?' I asked.

'After midday, Your Highness.'

'And what time is it now?' demanded Joan.

'Oh, it's early. The cooks are just going about their business. You've plenty of time to prepare to receive the king,' he said, examining our crumpled appearance.

'And have we missed Prime?' asked Joan.

'Yes, Your Highness. The garrison chaplain is strict about time. He expects everyone to be there before sunrise.'

'Oh, well. Should we decide what to wear, Berengaria?'

'Good idea. Alazne, see what's left in my baggage that is not too salty from the sea.'

'I'll go and look, and I'll set some things out in the sunshine. Does the sun always shine here, Hugo?'

'Yes, my lady, but there is always a shortage of water on the island.'

'I would not have believed that last night,' laughed Torène. 'We were drowning in it.'

We spent the rest of the morning getting ready while keeping out of sight of the sentries, who were using the ladder at the end of the corridor to access the roof.

Eventually, Alazne inspected me and pronounced me ready to meet my lord.

'What about you and Arrosa? Are you ready?' I asked.

'Nearly — we were preparing while we dressed you, Princess. Now, sit on the bed while we finish getting ready.'

They had hidden their gowns in Joan's chamber, so I tried to guess what would go with the burgundy gown that I was now wearing.

My hair had been left loose and was topped by a silver fillet encrusted with precious stones. My gown was open-necked, with a square halter edged with silver threads, and my arms were covered, of course, but the bodice was tight and my skirt flared out.

Joan wafted in when she was ready. She was dressed in gold and her hair was in a plait that reached her waist. On her head she wore a fine gauze headdress topped by a crown. The other women piled into my chamber; Alazne and Arrosa wore green gowns, while Pavot and Torène wore camocas gowns with gold and silver stripes.

'Ladies,' I said, 'you have done well, considering the circumstances. Are Queen Joan and I fit to receive a king?'

'Of course.'

'He should be pleased.'

'He is blessed.'

'Come on,' commanded Joan, 'let's take the air and wander down to the harbour while we await the return of my brother. Hugo's messengers will come and find us in good time, I expect.'

We made our way to the dusty castle forecourt, where we were immediately surrounded by the guard, its captain showing signs of distress.

'Your Highnesses, where are you going?' he asked. 'The town is not wholly safe.'

'Then come with us,' replied Joan, unfazed, 'and take some island air.'

'Yes, Your Highness,' he replied. He looked up at a sergeant peering over the parapet and raised his voice. 'Find Lord Hugo! Tell him we're going to…?'

'The harbour,' Joan informed him.

'The harbour!' he repeated, and then commanded six of his men to line up alongside us so we were fully protected from harm.

'The king will have my head if aught goes wrong, Your Highness,' he fretted as he strode alongside us.

The harbour had been brought into better order now, with the water clear and all galleys and ships safely moored. Stores and other items were lined up on the jetty ready for loading, and the crews sounded happy. Our guard captain encouraged us to take a look inside one of the warehouses at the end of the jetty. It was jammed full of every kind of booty: arms and armour, chests of coins, and banners.

'This is what the king's men captured from Isaac's army. There were a lot of horses too, left behind in stable lines when the Griffons fled from here. The king has kept Isaac's imperial standard, which he has decided to present to the Abbey of Saint Albans, in England.'

'How odd,' I ventured, 'so far away, yet he remembers an abbey. Why, Captain?'

'When Richard was a babe, he had a nurse to provide the comforts that are best provided by a mother —'

'He means a wet nurse,' clarified Joan.

'The woman was Hodierna of Saint Albans, and Richard shared her milk with her natural son, Alexander. Alexander is now a scholar and theologian at the Abbey of Saint Albans. Hodierna lives nearby still, and Richard provides her with a generous pension. This is a tribute to her, I believe — his first Crusade conquest.'

There was a shout from the direction of the castle. A youth was running towards us, kicking up clouds of dust.

'The king is coming, I'll warrant,' said the captain. 'Back to the castle, Your Highnesses.'

It was indeed the news that we had been waiting for, and the messenger boy confirmed it. The king's army was in sight.

Picking up our skirts, we set off at a trot. As we reached the steps up to the guard hall, there came another cry from above.

'Galleys on the horizon!'

'Where?' shouted the captain.

'To the east,' said the figure, peering over the parapet and pointing.

'Who can that be?' the captain wondered. 'Inside, Your Highnesses, if you please.'

'I want to go onto the roof, Captain,' I said.

'So do I,' added Joan.

'We'll all go,' said Pavot.

The captain shook his head and sighed. 'Sergeant!' he called to the guard. 'Take Their Highnesses onto the roof, and don't lose any of them. I've got things to attend to. Ah, here is Hugo. He can take care of you.'

Then he ran off onto the guard floor.

'Why has he left you here, Your Highnesses?' asked Hugo.

'He has things to do. There are ships approaching,' I explained.

'We are going up onto the roof to see them,' said Joan.

Hugo nodded. 'I wonder if the king has seen them? We will have a good view from up there.'

'Get yourself off and attend to your duties,' said Joan. 'We'll go up there ourselves.'

'Very well, Your Highness.' Hugo ran off towards the stables.

Scampering up the stairs as best we could in our gowns, we soon reached the bottom of the ladder leading to the roof. Hugo had sent two men-at-arms to help us, but normally we did not wear much beneath a gown. I looked at Joan, and she immediately understood the problem and turned to the metal giants beside us.

'You two, go and sit halfway down the stairs. Don't look up until we are all out on the roof,' she said.

The men grinned and replied, 'As you wish, Your Highness.'

Seeing them down at their new lookout post, I wondered what to do next.

'Hitch your skirts up into your belt,' instructed Joan.

Casting modesty aside, I did as advised and scuttled up the ladder. I dared not look down, and I finally managed to throw a foot over the hatch rim and plant it on the roof.

The sentries weren't expecting me and stood wide-eyed and silent as I peered back down the ladder.

'Next!' I called down. Then I asked the guards to point out the distant sails.

'There, Your Highness, slightly to your left,' indicated one.

'Look, Joan,' I said, when she arrived by my side.

'They're galleys,' added the soldier. 'You can see the oars flashing, Your Highness.'

'Oh yes,' she responded, 'but where is the king?'

'He was coming along the strand,' said the soldier, pointing to the distant shoreline, 'but when he saw those sails on the horizon, he turned round and set off back east — probably to meet them if they land. It was a bit chaotic, turning all his men around.'

'So if they are enemies, the king can catch them on the open sands,' said Joan.

'It may be that they will settle at Larnaca harbour, if they don't know that we're here further south, Your Highness.'

'What can I do?' I murmured.

'Wait, Princess,' said Joan. 'Start learning about being second in the kingdom. Back in Sicily, I once thought that I might be joint first, but I was not enough of an asset. Whatever occurs on the beach, Berengaria, you must be certain of your next step. Will you move onwards to Outremer and Jerusalem as a queen, or return to Navarre as a princess?'

'Joan, I am Jerusalem-bound and shall become the Queen of England and the wife of the Lionheart, of that have no doubt,' I said firmly.

She smiled and took my hand as we turned our attention to the distant shore. 'With God's blessing,' she added.

CHAPTER FOURTEEN

After a while, Joan and Arrosa led me across the roof to look down into the castle yard. A great marquee was now fully erected, and Hugo and his staff were all rushing around.

'See, Berengaria, they know that the king is coming,' said Joan.

'Well, I can't see him,' I said petulantly.

'I can, Your Highness,' called one of the sentries. 'Look yonder.'

He pointed to the far end of the great curving bay of Lemesós. I could see tiny figures, which must have been Richard and his army, the sails having disappeared over the horizon.

'How far is that, soldier?' asked Joan.

'About three miles, Your Highness. They're only just visible, but that must be the king with all those banners and flags. Never fear, they will be back here before you know it.'

'Oh, good,' I sniffed, unconvinced.

'The roof!' someone called from the yard below.

'Captain?' a sentry shouted down.

'Can you see what's happening?'

'Aye, lord, the king's coming near. Those galleys have gone away.'

It was Hugo shouting up next. 'Your Highnesses, I'll continue with preparations for the feast, shall I?'

'Please do!' Joan shouted back. She grinned at me. 'One way or another, we are going to cheer you up, Princess.'

'How do we get down off this roof?' asked Alazne.

Overhearing us, one of the sentries replied, 'Do not fret, we'll help you onto the ladder one by one. If you'll allow us to hold your hands, that is?'

I faced him and replied, 'Thank you, you are most kind. I shall commend you to your captain.'

Leading us to the hatch, he peered down the ladder and shouted, 'Pierre, go down those stairs, and make sure that nobody comes up them!' After a moment of peering, he invited me to go over the edge.

Soon we were all off the roof and wondering what to do next.

'Let's tidy up,' said Alazne. 'Climbing up ladders has done nothing for your regal appearance, Princess.'

Joan and I inspected each other and burst out laughing.

'Well spotted, Alazne,' said Joan. 'Shall we smarten up and go outside? There is lots going on.'

Soon we were in the castle yard. Strings of war horses were waiting near the stables.

'Your Highnesses,' greeted Hugo when he spotted us looking at these powerful beasts, 'these horses are some of the prizes that the king has captured.'

'Yes, but where is the king?' I asked.

'The sentries will hail when they spot him, Your Highness.'

'We'll need to wait,' said Joan. 'Show us into the marquee, Hugo. You said that we would be feasting in there.'

He led us into the colourful tent. Tables were set out in two lines with one great table across the top, and in its centre were two thrones. All the table surfaces were covered with white linen and decorated with candelabrum and dishes of gold and silver. Gold and silver models of animals were also placed at intervals along the centre of the tables. Tall, church-like candle posts were set along the floor between the line of tables leading towards the top, and above our heads hung the banners of those lords taking part in the Crusade.

'Hugo,' exclaimed Joan, 'you have done well. Fit for a king, indeed!'

'And two queens, I hope,' I said.

'Where are we sitting?' asked Alazne.

'Behind the thrones, ladies. You are not forgotten,' answered Hugo. There was indeed a small eating area set up behind the top table, curtained off by a flimsy chiffon drape.

'You will be attended at table, ladies, and from there you will be able to see and hear all that transpires. There is also a rear entrance, which will be used to service the king's table, and through which you may escape when the conversation becomes too bawdy. Your Highnesses, you will be the judge of when that time is reached, I trust.'

I thought of something else. 'Is there to be music, Hugo? We can't have a feast without music.'

'Your Highness! Dear me, I had not thought of that, but what can I do? I only have soldiers and sailors, not musicians.'

'But we have,' I said. 'Our sailors have instruments on board the *Dione*, and I'm certain that is how they entertain when not busy with sails and things.'

'I'll send for your musicians and instruments from the *Dione*.'

'Thank you. Then you can leave the rest to me,' I said. Here was something that I could do to help; a bit of music always brought good cheer.

'Lord Hugo!' There was a shout from outside the pavilion, and a soldier poked his head through the doorway. 'The king is near — a mile, no more.'

'Excellent, call out the guard captain and ask him to line up the garrison.' He smiled at me. 'It seems that your betrothed has finally arrived, Your Highness. And if I remember, the king is a singer and a poet and has a love of music. You might just have suggested something that will please him.' He smiled and bowed before moving off to the entrance.

'Let's go outside and join the welcoming throng,' said Joan.

The heat was overwhelming, and I thought that the troops who had lined up from the castle steps to the end of the road near the harbour must have been dripping with sweat even after a few minutes.

A trumpet sounded from the top of the castle, signalling that the king was close. The watching crowd was being held back by the line of men-at-arms, and their murmurs swelled.

'I can hear horses,' exclaimed Alazne.

The ground began to shake and a cheer from the crowd round the corner confirmed Richard's approach. Then he appeared at last, a proud general at the head of his triumphant army. The noise was tremendous as the lines of cavalry and then the marching troops appeared rank by rank. Then the smells hit me: horse droppings, oiled metal and men's sweat.

'Aha!' Richard halted in front of us. The sun was behind him, and he appeared in silhouette, high in the saddle, but I could discern the shape of his crown on top of his helm.

'Come down, brother, and give your sister a hug and your betrothed a kiss,' said Joan.

'I can do that.' A groom appeared to hold the reins of his horse, and the king vaulted off its back to land in front of us with a dusty thud.

Joan got the first embrace, and then Richard turned his attention to me.

'Berengaria.' He went onto one knee, and I held my breath, wondering what was coming next. 'How would you like to be the Queen of England and the Damsel of Cyprus?'

'What about Isaac Comnenus?' I asked.

Standing, Richard embraced me and I even got a little brush on the lips. 'Comnenus has fled to Nicosia. Cyprus will be mine,' he said with pride. 'And you, my dear Berengaria, will become the first lady, the Damsel of Cyprus.'

'May I begin by becoming your queen, my lord?'

'Ha! A queen with spirit. Yes, we'll get that done.'

'Whose ships delayed you, brother?' asked Joan.

'Those were carrying the King of Jerusalem, Guy de Lusignan. He is in some bother. Philip wants rid of him in favour of someone else, and Guy has come to plead for help. He will go on to Famagusta to wait there for me; we shall join him later. It is no impediment to our wedding, dear Berengaria.' He looked over me and spied Hugo. 'So, who's in charge here now? Hugo, tell me what has been happening.'

'Your Highness, since my services did not please you on the field of battle, I have taken to organising the castle in your absence.'

'Hugo, Hugo, fret not. You are not the only one to offer me advice. I listen but I must follow my instincts. So what have you done here?'

'We have the soldiers and sailors from the vessels that were wrecked on the shore. They were taken prisoner by the Griffons, but they overpowered their guards and fought valiantly to rid the town of them.'

'Soldiers! Are these the ones lined up?'

'Yes, Your Highness, and their captain is at the end there. You may care to meet him later. The sailors have been turned into castle servants; they have erected these marquees with their seaman's crafts and have taken on a lot of the other castle duties. Providing I keep the wine store locked, they are an asset and have worked hard.'

'Yes, yes. Berengaria, you are looking splendid. What do you think about being a queen and a lady all at once?'

'I've done many things since I left my palace at Olite. I'll try another, Richard. We'll try it together, if you wish?'

'Ha! Hear that? If I could recruit more like her, we'd soon rule the world.'

He came close again and placed his hands on my shoulders. My nose must have wrinkled, because a light came into his eyes.

'Hugo, is there a bathing chamber in this castle of yours? I believe I offend some nostrils hereabouts.' He grinned at me.

'Better than that, Your Highness; there is a full bathhouse in the Byzantine style, and they are ready for you.'

'Splendid, splendid. I'll see you later, Joan, Berengaria.'

Once they had left, Hugo said, 'If Your Highnesses would care to retire to your chambers, out of the heat, I'll come and fetch you when the king is ready to dine.'

'Suits me,' I agreed. 'You'd best catch up with the king; he has long legs.'

We began to make our way to our chambers.

'Tell me what you know about Guy de Lusignan,' I said to Joan.

She scoffed. 'Without Jerusalem, he is no king. And as I understand it, he is only king by right of marriage; he married Sibylla, widow of King Baldric. Lusignan's past actions made this Crusade necessary. He lost a battle at a place known as the Horns of Hattin, after which Saladin — the leader of the Saracen army — presented himself outside the walls of Jerusalem. Sibylla and a knight known as Balian d'Ibelin, who had been left behind as the garrison commander, accepted terms from Saladin, and Balian was free to march away from the Holy City.'

'I have heard this,' I said, 'but not in such detail. Lusignan was spared by Saladin.'

'Indeed. Some other leaders were not. One named Raynard, who had been active in promoting conflict against Saladin, was beheaded publicly by Saladin himself as an "oath-breaker". Lusignan was held prisoner for a year until Sibylla managed to persuade Saladin to give him back.'

'They were in communication?'

'So it seems — I expect that emissaries come and go. It does not prevent them plotting, though, and sending messages with spears and arrows.'

'So what does Guy de Lusignan want of Richard?'

'Support, I suppose. He has come from Akko, which is under siege. Sibylla died last July, as did her daughters — it was some pestilence. It flourishes over there.'

'Leaving his kingship in doubt,' I murmured. 'How do you come by this information?'

'Hugo. He is a fount of knowledge.'

'I see that I should question him more often. Anything else?'

'Yes. The High Court, the Haute Cour of Jerusalem and a lot of the barons are still against Lusignan because of Hattin — and he has not been able to take Akko. They want a different king, Conrad of Montferrat. They have married him off to Sibylla's half-sister Isabella: it is a strange line of descent, from queen-sister to sister, but it makes Conrad eligible to be king if Lusignan were to die.'

'This sounds interesting, Joan. I can't wait to get to the Holy Land.' We had arrived at the stairs to our chambers. 'Up the stairs, ladies, we've some dance steps to practise.'

With the chamber floor cleared, I stood ready to begin. Flanked by Alazne and Arrosa, but lacking musicians, I looked to Joan and her women to provide a beat.

'Sit on the bed together, you three, and stamp your feet and clap like this.' I clapped out the rhythm with my hands. 'One, two, three; one, two, three, four — one, two, three; one, two, three, four. Good, now faster.'

They soon mastered the correct rhythm and speed.

I turned to Alazne and Arrosa. 'Now, ladies, the fandango.' With my hands on my hips and my shoes cast off, I called the time. Soon we were whirling, and soon there were curious faces in the doorway. We cared not, for an audience improved the dancing. The clapping increased until it must have been heard throughout the castle.

It did not take us long to regain our long-practised ability to perform the dance of our homeland.

'That was wonderful,' said Joan. 'I had not thought that I was musical, in the way that Richard is, but you have shown us how to enjoy it too. Thank you, Berengaria.'

Panting a little, we settled on my bed. Having been reminded of my homeland, I now wished to asked Joan about her previous kingdom.

'In all the time we've been travelling together, Joan, you've not told us why you left your realm. You are still Queen of Sicily, are you not?'

'That might be a matter for debate. You told me what happened at Lodi, but now we are short of news. The only certain thing is that I am the queen dowager, and Tancred is the king.'

'Did he pay King Richard to get you out of the way?' asked Alazne. I thought this question might be a touch intrusive, but Joan answered without rancour.

'Probably, yes. The story will come out eventually, but you might as well hear it from me.' She hesitated. 'I'll begin with my marriage to the previous king of Sicily, William. I was thirteen when we wed. He didn't press for any intimate attentions, and I thought that he was being kind. He let me have my own palace, and we were on good terms. I was happy, riding and hawking. I knew that one day we would try to produce an heir, but there seemed to be time.'

'Sounds odd,' I said. 'Was he interested in men?'

'No, that was not the problem. When we did bed, when I was fifteen, everything was as expected. Like most things it needed practice, but after a while William began to leave me alone.'

'Was he horrid to you?' asked Arrosa.

'No — he was always polite.'

'He had a private palace in the grounds,' said Pavot. 'Except it was not a real palace.'

'No,' said Joan ruefully, 'it was his harem.'

'What happened, Joan?' I asked. 'How did you find out?'

'He went away for the day. He had always told me that the building was where his clothes makers worked, so I went to have a small fault in a gown repaired. They wouldn't let me in at first, but I insisted, as the queen. There were seamstresses and suchlike working in the front of the hall, but they all kept looking at some curtains at the back, so I pushed my way in, and…'

She broke off, tears in her eyes. I put my arm around her, and Arrosa found a small cloth for her to dry her eyes; this was going to be difficult. When she was composed, she continued.

'It was a long corridor with chambers off it. I went along, pushing open the doors or pulling open the curtains, and every chamber had a young woman and a bed in it. I began to speak to them. They were from all over Europe, Asia, and Africa. William had sent out agents to procure them for him; they were all slaves, bought for his pleasure.'

'William was a debauched slaver,' added Pavot, 'and it got worse.'

Joan nodded. 'When he returned, he was told that I had found him out. He came storming in, accusing me of interfering in his affairs and telling me that I was untrustworthy.'

'What did you do?' I asked, kissing her on the cheek.

'I was furious, lacking control. I told him that he was a traitor to his Christian vows and a moral deviant. I threw things at him and swore that he would never again come near me, and that I would go back to Aquitaine.'

'What did he do?'

'He stormed off. I didn't see him for two days. Then he came to me; he wanted to apologise and he promised to free the women.'

'Did you agree?' asked Arrosa.

'I told him that I had a letter for Richard in safekeeping, and that if he didn't reform, I would have it sent.'

At that moment, Hugo came to the door; it was time to attend the king's supper party.

'Have you found me some musicians, Hugo?' I asked.

'Indeed I have, Your Highness. Will six do — three from your ship and three assorted seamen?'

'Yes, and a practice chamber. It won't take long.'

'For tonight?'

'No, there's no time now. But for the wedding.'

'Ah!' he said, eyes bright. 'Music for a wedding, splendid.'

Holding Joan's hand, I led her down the steps and along a brazier-lit pathway to the grand marquee.

'There are other tents ready now, Your Highnesses. That one over there is the king's.'

'Oh,' said Joan, 'are we moving out?'

'No, Your Highness. It remains safer for you at the top of the castle. Please remain there, if you would.'

The king's pavilion was nearby, down a well-lit path, but we made our way to the back entrance of the marquee, and Hugo took us into an anteroom. The main part of the tent could be seen through thin gauze curtains, and we found ourselves on the other side of the screen we had seen earlier.

'If you wait here, this is where you ladies will be sitting.' Our ladies looked around. It was very nicely set up with a specially laid out table for them. 'When the king emerges from his pavilion, he will enter here; then Your Highnesses can go through to the main chamber with him. I can get you a drink now, if you wish.'

I soon had a glass of Cypriot wine in my hand as we watched Richard's other guests arrive.

At that moment, Hugo waved a white cloth through the curtain and a trumpet blast assailed my ears. From behind, the canvas door was pulled back and someone announced, 'King Richard!'

He came in behind us and I gasped at the sight. He wore a red tunic with three lions emblazoned on the front, white breeches and soft shoes, but the most striking part was his head. His golden-red locks reached his shoulders, and his penetrating grey eyes were set off by his red beard and moustaches, which had been skilfully trimmed.

'Joan, Berengaria,' he boomed, 'those baths were excellent.' He looked at me. 'I will not cause you to recoil tonight. A kiss for your lord, eh?' He bent and dwelled softly upon my yielding lips.

'We are ready, Your Highness,' said Hugo.

'Still in charge, I see. We'll have to appoint a proper constable — we can't have clerks doing the job. But you are doing splendidly; I'm most grateful. Come, Berengaria, take my hand. Joan, by my side. Hugo, the curtains.'

Hugo waved his cloth and the muslin was swept back to let us receive another trumpet blast from the other end of the canvas hall.

'That'll have the walls of Jericho down!' cried Richard. 'Come, Princess.'

I walked to the table with my betrothed, while Hugo led Joan to the chair to the right of Richard. We wouldn't be able to speak to each other now. I noted that Hugo had made sure that I had a throne with high legs, so that my head was only a little below Richard's.

'Right, Berengaria,' said Richard, 'that tall fellow standing behind us is Mercadier. He's in charge of the mercenaries that I employ to keep my head on my shoulders, at a great cost.'

I looked round. Mercadier was enormous, with a black beard and eyebrows, and he was festooned with weapons of all descriptions. His eyes were wandering constantly around the tent.

'That fellow, first on that table —' Richard indicated the long table on our right — 'is my cavalry marshal, Hugh of Poitiers. A fine horseman. Do you ride, Berengaria?'

'Gladly, and as often as I can. I am a skilled horsewoman.'

'And modest. Hear that, Poitiers? I've found you a riding partner. Take her out and see what she's made of.'

'With pleasure.' He smiled at me and I nodded.

'Next to him is Robert, Earl of Leicester.'

Another handsome lord, I thought, and smiled.

'First on that table on our left is Jean, Bishop of Evreux — a nice fellow.'

The bishop was a bit older than everybody else and he seemed like a pleasant man, but he surprised me with his greeting. 'Is everything ready for the morning, Princess Berengaria?' he asked.

'Tomorrow?' I raised my eyebrows.

'Oh, sorry, Berengaria, I forgot to mention that the wedding is tomorrow,' said Richard. 'Haven't got much time, you see — got to bring that fellow Isaac to heel. Are you doing anything tomorrow? I'd like to marry you, if you still wish.'

I felt my smile tighten. Mother of God, there was no way back now. 'This, my lord, is why I have travelled all this way, to hear you say that. Of course. What time?'

'Ha! Hear that, Hugh? You'll have to put off tomorrow's ride out — we're getting married.' He stood up. 'Quiet, listen to this.' The pavilion hushed. 'There will be a wedding tomorrow; the princess has agreed.'

He raised his goblet to the loudest cheer I had ever heard, and then the feast began.

'Saint Pancras's day, Princess Berengaria,' said the stout bishop. 'Patron saint of young people; he got beheaded when he was fourteen.'

'Who did that?' I asked.

'Romans, in the year of our Lord 304. Emperor Diocletian: a nasty man who is burning in hell, I'd suppose.'

Having been told about the wedding, I was not very hungry and ate little. I caught Joan's eye from time to time, but her eyes wandered about. She tried to show interest in the bishop and the other lords bold enough to try and engage with her, but Richard concentrated on me and my admirers.

Everybody wanted to talk to me. Some came up to the table and spoke to Richard, but they had their eyes on me as they did so — it was a bit like home, but more intense. I supposed that I'd get used to it when I was a queen.

The final well-wisher came as I began to yawn. The need to say something polite in response to every enquiry was tiring — though not as tiring as Richard's occasional compliments. I was unable to ask him a single question. It was as if he was keeping me at arm's length.

Then Joan presented us with the opportunity to leave. Turning to Richard, she whispered something in his ear and he looked at me.

'It will become a bit bawdy now, sweet one, if you want to leave. Take Joan with you, please,' he said.

'Thank you, Richard, I am a bit tired,' I said. 'What time is the wedding tomorrow?'

'When we're both ready. There's lots to organise. I'll send Hugo to see you first thing, and then we'll agree a time to suit us. No hurry, we've got all day. Give me a kiss.'

I kissed him, and then he stood up and banged on the table.

'Queen Joan of Sicily and Princess Berengaria of Navarre are leaving!' he bawled.

The men stood up, some struggling with wine-weakened knees, and then we were chased out of the hall by those annoying trumpets. Our ladies joined us as we quit the grand pavilion.

'What did you say, Joan, to get us out of there?'

'I said that I needed to visit the garderobe.'

'Good, for I really do. Let's get a message to Hugo and find out where the musicians are. We'll have a dance practice first thing tomorrow. You can lead it, ladies, and show them the steps. See if those sailors can pick it up.'

'Oh, yes, how exciting,' gushed Arrosa. Alazne was subdued, but I needed to put that to the back of my mind. They both went to carry out my orders.

'How am I going to sleep tonight, Joan?' I asked.

'I'll stay with you and talk you to sleep.'

When we arrived at my chamber, I lay on my bed, not bothering to undress. Joan sat beside me, and I rested my head on her lap until Alazne and Arrosa returned.

'Are we having music?'

'We are,' said Alazne. 'They are all delighted. I found them playing on the guard floor. The *Dione*'s people are leading the other sailors in a merry dance.'

Joan laughed. 'Well done, Alazne. I can only imagine you ladies playing to a sailor's tune.'

'You'll only need to wait until morning, Your Highness.'

'Tell us more about your William, Joan. Did you ever lie with him again?' I asked. I needed to explore the world of marriage; it seemed a mysterious state for those outside of it.

'Oh, that. I decided to remain aloof until I was certain of his intentions. He was a most beautiful man, but I doubt I ever loved him truly. He was a bit of a peacock, with no real substance. He had other women, lots of them, but he couldn't have loved them. They were not free to choose him; he just used them.'

'I heard that there was a child, Joan. Is it true?'

'Yes, I was the only one who could give him an heir. My body was necessary to him, and his mother pleaded his case.'

'Margaret of Navarre. She's my great-aunt,' I said. 'I never met her, of course; she was married off when but a child.'

'She was a very strong woman, and very persistent. I conceived, but there must have been something wrong: God's will was that the child should not survive. We fell apart then, and he fell ill and died soon afterwards.'

'That's so sad,' I said, squeezing her hand.

I lay for a while before I went to sleep, dwelling on Joan's story.

When I woke, I was still propped up by Joan and Alazne, who were still asleep.

Pavot was at the end of the bed, grinning at me. 'It's time to rise, Your Highnesses. The sun is shining.'

'Is my gown laid out?' I asked.

Alazne groaned as she woke up. 'Look over there. Arrosa hung it out last night.'

Then I heard Hugo calling from the corridor. 'Good morning, Your Highnesses. May I talk with the princess, please?'

'Of course, Hugo, speak,' I said.

'Privately, Your Highness, if you please.'

'We'll go to my chamber,' said Joan. 'Come on, ladies.' She led them out.

Hugo led me to a corner and lowered his voice. 'The king has asked me to talk to you, princess. He makes it clear that it is a matter of some delicacy, but you are not to blame for it, so be absolved from what I am about to convey to you.'

I waited, giving him no help.

'It's the dancing, Your Highness, and the gay music. His Highness would like you to reconsider it, on account of the vow of the cross. Many of his senior knights, his great lords and of course the many priests and bishops who are attending the wedding have taken the vow.'

I waited still. There was something else hovering.

'Some have included chastity in the vow, as with the Knights Templar, Your Highness.'

I started, alarmed. 'And Richard?'

'He did not say, Your Highness, but as he has not halted the ceremony, I assume not.'

I sat on my bed to think. Surely Richard was going to bed me tonight, if he wished for a son. I could not conjure a miraculous conception.

Hugo, ever sensitive, broke into my thoughts. 'The spectacle of dancing ladies might tempt some to break their vows, you see?'

I burst out laughing. There were tears running down my face by the time Joan, Arrosa and Alazne came running back, all with anxious faces.

'What is it, Berengaria?' asked Joan. 'What has my brother done now?'

'Nothing much,' I replied, wiping away the tears. 'Your dear brother is afraid for the souls of his lords and some bishops. It seems that the dancing is off for fear that these gallant knights might struggle with their celibacy and that bishop's heads may be filled with impure thoughts.'

'What should I say, Your Highness?' asked Hugo, blushing.

'Why does he not tell me about this himself?'

'He is in conference with Bishop Jean of Evreux, and he is trying to get dressed for the ceremony. There is a queue of nobles outside his tent, all desperate to ask him questions about the war, Your Highness. He is hard pressed at the moment.'

Ignoring the laughter behind me, I said, 'Tell the king that we will refrain from dancing if he will permit music. I cannot be wed in the atmosphere of a funeral. And have some food sent up. I'm famished.'

This cheered him and he trotted off to try his luck with the king. Then, while we composed ourselves and began choosing embellishments for our dress, a procession of youths galloped up the stairs, carrying platters and flagons.

'Joan, do you know if Richard's taken the vow of the cross?' I asked.

'The vow? Yes, he took it in 1187 when he was made Count of Poitiers, and again at his coronation in England, September 1189.'

'Did he include the vow of chastity?'

'I don't know. His son was born in 1180, but after that I was in Sicily.'

Now I was worried. Joan put her arm around me and Alazne came across, eating bread and cheese.

'What's wrong, Your Highnesses?' she asked. 'Is there a problem?'

Joan hurriedly explained, and then went on, 'Richard needs an heir, Berengaria. Mother wouldn't have dragged you all the way here if there was no possibility of that. I'm certain that all will be well, and if it isn't you can always divorce him. I'll support you, and it'll serve him right. Mother will be furious.'

'I'm going to see him,' I said. 'Come with me, Joan.'

Without bothering to change out of our nightgowns, we left the chamber. When we reached Richard's tent, no one got in our way. Some half-hearted attempt to impede me was made by Mercadier, but the look in my eye put him off. I was left to throw back the curtain of his tent and march in.

'Berengaria!' Richard exclaimed.

'Your Highness!' added Jean, Bishop of Evreux.

'I need some assurance,' I demanded.

'Oh,' said Jean, smiling. 'I'll leave you two for a moment. Reassure the lady, Richard. You should have done this earlier.' He left, tutting to himself.

'Is it about our wedding night?' asked Richard.

'What makes you think that?'

'Oh, rumours abound in such a small place,' he smiled.

Joan also pushed her way in. 'What are you doing, Richard?' she demanded.

'By the sins of Beelzebub, you sound like Mother. If you calm down, I'll explain. There's nothing to worry about. Please, sit.' He indicated a chair and drew up another in front of me. Joan stood behind with her hands on my shoulders. Richard took my hands in his. 'I did take the vow of chastity. I gave up a lot; I have forsaken many friends to take the vow of the cross and dedicate my life to the Lord, until the city of Jerusalem is once more back in the hands of Christians.'

'Friends? Or women?'

'Both. I have abstained from the pleasures of the flesh and done penance at times to atone for the sins of my previous life, but...' He squeezed my hands and gazed earnestly at me. 'Mother Church also understands the needs of temporal authority and desires of the state. I need an heir, as you well know, Berengaria.'

'So how do you propose to achieve that, Richard?' demanded Joan.

He smiled. 'Bishop Jean was here for just that purpose. He has granted us a dispensation. For one day from when we are confirmed as man and wife, we will be free to pursue whatever is necessary to achieve our desires.' He stood, still holding my hands, and pulled me up to face him. 'If you agree.'

'And after that short rutting season, what then?' asked his sister.

'The sooner Jerusalem is released from the grip of the Saracens, the sooner we can resume our activities.'

'Mother of God! Is there any wine in here?' I gasped.

'Yes, yes. I'll join you, if I may.'

Richard went across to a buffet table and busied himself pouring out some wine. I stood with Joan alongside me, who held my hand and talked softly.

'He is making a huge sacrifice for the Church. It is up to you: will you go along with him and give him some support? God knows he needs it.'

'That is a very persuasive argument. It is true that those who assist the liberation of the Holy City in any way will receive indulgences, but I cannot guarantee a result after one night.'

'True, but as he has told you, once the city is freed...'

'Fornication from dusk to dawn. Yes, I know.'

Richard came and stood next to us. 'Here you are. I drink to your health. Have you made up your mind, Berengaria? You did say that you liked an adventure.'

I looked him up and down. He towered over me, still in his long night attire. 'We won't be interrupted after the wedding? I can't have folk visiting while we are seeking to maintain your dynasty.'

He nodded. 'We are to have a private boudoir in a tent. It will be in the olive orchard, away from all the fuss and revelry — I assure you that we will not be disturbed. You won't mind occupying a tent, will you? It is only for one night.'

'My pleasure.'

'Then we are agreed, one wedding, one crowning, then one night of love. Is that adventure enough for you, Berengaria?'

I nodded, and he bent down and kissed me. It was long and gentle, and then passion came. I grasped him around the neck.

Richard broke off and lifted me above his head, grinning.

'Not now, there's a wedding first,' Joan reminded us. 'Come on, Berengaria. Let's leave before the king's soul falls into the fires of hell.'

We made our way back to my bedchamber.

'Gowns, ladies!' I cried.

Hugo was still there. 'There is one more thing for you, Princess,' he said. 'The king has been advised to include a Saxon tradition during the ceremony.'

'England being full of them, I suppose,' said Joan.

'Indeed. It is the custom to exchange gifts as tokens of love.'

'What manner of gift, Hugo?' I asked.

'This will suffice.' He offered me a gold ring with a gleaming red stone set in it.

'That's a costly item. Where did you come by it, Hugo?' asked Joan.

'In the castle vaults, Your Highness. It probably belongs to Comnenus.'

I gave it to Joan. 'Can you be by my side and carry this for me?' I asked.

'I would be honoured, dear Berengaria.'

'Well done, Hugo. You have saved us some embarrassment.' I planted a kiss upon his cheek and he blushed. I turned to my ladies. 'Let's have a look at this gown, Alazne.'

It was wine-coloured silk. The neck was level with my armpits and it sat close around my upper body, leaving space for ornaments between my bosom and throat. The bodice was embellished with full lacing across my chest, and the skirt swept out, embroidered with pearls. There was also a white chiffon mantle with bouffant sleeves down to the elbows, with gold edging on the cuffs. I had a gold chain with a ruby pendant to wear around my neck, and I would have a chiffon veil upon my head when I left the chamber. My ladies worked gold threads into my hair, which they fashioned into a wide braid that almost reached my waist. Then they stood around me to view their work.

'Well?' I said with some annoyance.

'Beautiful,' answered Joan. 'If Richard can't see that, then I'm off to Aquitaine, for this Crusade has become an obsession.'

'Joan!' I said, shocked. 'That is God's work. I can only come after Richard's duties.'

'Maybe I have had enough of duties. I'll be proud to escort you into church, as all I've done so far is get you into a storm, a shipwreck and a war that we did not expect.'

I took her hand and kissed it. 'We have had an entirely wonderful time with you to guide us, have we not, ladies?'

'Yes,' agreed Arrosa with enthusiasm.

'Yes,' muttered Alazne, with less.

'Now it is your turn to dress. By the way, Joan, what are you wearing?'

'It is a secret. Pavot and Torène have rifled through my chests to find some matching outfits. You'll have to wait until we are ready.' She flounced across the corridor and the door to her bedchamber was gently closed behind her.

I watched as Arrosa and Alazne began to dress. First, each put on a white blouse with puffed sleeves, then a red kirtle and a black sleeveless bolero, buttoned up with two rows of pearl buttons. They also each wore a linen cap and Roman lace-up sandals. Every piece had been made by hand in Navarre.

We waited for Joan to emerge from her side of the corridor.

Hugo came trotting up the stairs. 'Are you ready, Your Highness?'

'Almost,' I replied.

'Please go down to the guard floor until the herald summons us, then wait until I call you forth. The church bell will toll, and that's when you move; it will keep ringing while you make your way round the castle and enter the church of Saint George. Your captain, Javier, will meet you down in the guard hall and provide an escort of six to accompany you. After the wedding, you will come back to the guard hall for the crowning. Where is Queen Joan?'

'We're coming, Hugo. Do not fret.'

Joan's door was thrown open and she emerged, supported by Pavot and Torène. Once more, she was dressed entirely in gold. Her gown had a full skirt and close-fitting sleeves, and she wore a gold necklace, gold bracelets and gold rings. Her hair was loose and topped by a crown and a sheer headdress.

Hugo gasped and dashed downstairs again.

'There's enough gold on display to pay for Richard's Crusade, I daresay,' said Alazne.

Joan smiled, and it lit up the chamber.

CHAPTER FIFTEEN

The guard hall was crowded with folk eager to catch a glimpse of us. Hugo came bustling in though the main door and breathed a sigh of relief when he saw us there. 'It is nearly midday, Your Highnesses. The bell's toll is not far away. But prepare yourselves; the king has issued pardons to all the local citizens, and they have come back out of hiding from the hills, orchards and secret places. It seems that they are all pressed into the castle yard, waiting for your appearances.'

'Oh dear,' said Joan. 'This has become a very public affair.'

'This is not surprising, Your Highness, since the princess is to become the Damsel of Cyprus in a very short time.'

'Oh, has Emperor Isaac handed over power, Hugo?' I asked.

He looked at me strangely before answering. 'Not yet, Your Highness. The king is going into the hills to find Isaac as soon as he may; he will inform him of the change in circumstances.'

Joan laughed. 'My brother's version of diplomacy, Hugo?'

'Indeed, Your Highness.'

The bell tolled once. It was time to go.

I saw Javier standing in the doorway, looking fine in full armour. He waved his sword at me and called, 'The church is full of bishops, Your Highness. It is like the gates of heaven.'

The bell began its summoning peal and Joan's hand tightened around mine. As we came nearer to the door, the light and heat began to reach me. When we emerged, the crowd shouted out a hallelujah, the trumpeters who were posted on either side of the door blasted their tribute, and the full heat of the sun fell upon me.

'Follow me,' mouthed Javier, and he led us down the steps into the yard. We moved along the castle wall to the garrison chapel of Saint George, where there was a sudden change of atmosphere.

Javier could come no further, for no arms were permitted inside the church. As my eyes adjusted to the dim light, the noise of the crowd was left behind and I heard a gentle voice nearby.

'I am Father Nicolas, chaplain to His Highness. Please follow me to the altar, Your Highness.'

The chapel was full of finely dressed men, dimly visible through the smoke from the incense.

As I neared the altar, I saw Richard. He was wearing a tunic of rose-coloured samite and a silk mantle, which was embroidered with silver half-moons. On his head he wore a scarlet cap embroidered along the edge with gold lions. Beneath his tunic were white breeches, and on his feet were soft red slippers, also embroidered with lions. His long golden-red hair reached his shoulders and was topped by the crown of England.

Smiling, he held out a hand. I took it, and as we turned to face the altar, I received gracious smiles from the Archbishop of Bayonne and the Bishops of Apamea and Auxerre. Then Jean of Evreux began his reading from the Gospel according to Matthew.

The bishop held his hand upon my head and murmured a Latin blessing, and then he did the same to Richard.

Looking at the king, he asked, 'Do you have a gift to present to Her Highness?'

'I do,' he replied as Robert, Earl of Leicester handed Richard a ring.

'And do you, Your Highness, have a token of your love to exchange with Richard?'

'I do,' I replied, taking the ring handed me by Joan.

'Richard, do you give freely this token of your love to Berengaria?'

'I do,' he responded. He took my hand and placed his ring on the only finger that it would fit. 'This is an homage to the English custom of marriage, for you are now the Queen of England.' He lowered his voice. 'We'll change it later,' he whispered. 'It's all I could find.'

'Berengaria, do you give freely this token of your love to Richard?' asked Bishop Jean.

'I do,' I said.

'Then may the blessing of our Lord be upon you and bless your union. *In nomine Patris et Filii et Spiritus Sancti.*'

Richard bent down and kissed me gently. 'We must move for the next bit. Our thrones await; will you sit upon your throne, Queen Berengaria? Bishop Jean has a need to anoint us.'

'Yes, my lord.'

Javier and his six men escorted Bishop Jean from the little church back to the castle, amid the cheering crowds. Richard and I followed, closely guarded by Captain Mercadier and six of his men. In the guard hall, we were met by another blast from the trumpeters, lined up on the stairs to the upper floors now, no doubt to surprise us once more, which they did. An avenue of bodies, mostly lords and knights, opened up before us, at the end of which were two thrones.

Bishop Jean occupied the space between the thrones and turned to watch us approach. I was directed to sit on the left, and Richard sat on the right. The bishop held up a crown, almost as big as the one that Richard was wearing. He was wafted with incense by two priests waving censers, and although the guard hall was not as smoky as the church had been, it still caused many to cough a little.

Then the bishop began his next oration, addressing it to me. 'O God, who providest for Thy people by Thy power and rulest over them in love; grant unto this Thy servant Berengaria our queen, the spirit of wisdom and government, that being devoted unto Thee with all her heart, she may so wisely support the kingdom of her husband, Richard, that in his time Thy Church and people may continue in safety and prosperity, and that, persevering in good works unto the end, she may through Thy mercy come to Thine everlasting kingdom; through Jesus Christ Thy Son our Lord. Amen.' He held the crown high above my head. 'Do you, Berengaria, accept and swear to the acceptance of this sacred charge?'

'I do.'

He lowered the crown upon my head. As he took away his hands, he dipped a thumb into a small basin of oil — held out by yet another bishop — and called out, '*Sit laus Berengariam per voluntatem Dei ex Anglia reginae.*'

A great shout came back from the crowd gathered within the guard, which was repeated by those elsewhere as the event was relayed to them.

'*Sit laus Reginam Berengariam.*'

I risked turning my head to see Richard grinning at me. 'Where did you get this crown from?'

'Hugo found it in the vault. It is the empress's crown.'

'Was she very big?'

'Despair not, my queen, it fits you fair.'

'By God's grace, this thing will not fall off, Richard.'

'Well, keep still. The bishop is coughing again.'

Bishop Jean began his next pronouncement. '*Ave Berengariam, per gratiam Dei, domina Cypri.*'

There was another great trumpeting, and once more the crowds sang my praises.

'I'll be deaf if this continues!' I shouted in Richard's ear. 'Have you got anything else planned that I know nothing about?'

'Possibly, but we only made up these ceremonies this morning. There has not been enough time. Remember that this has never been done in this way before — we are unique in Christendom, Berengaria.'

'That much is clear.'

'There is more — have you forgotten your dower?'

'Yes, what is it?'

'Are the charters ready?' Richard asked of the bishop.

'Indeed, Your Highness.' He gestured to a side table, where some witnesses were gathered and upon which a large sheet of vellum lay.

'I shall read out the details, Your Highnesses, if you will permit,' said the king's clerk, Phillip of Poitou, and he received a nod from Richard.

By the time he reached the end, I had become the Duchess of Normandy and Aquitaine in waiting, Countess of Anjou and Maine, which included the castles and towns of Le Mans, Falaise, Domfront, Bonneville-sur-Touques and various other towns in Maine and Poitou, most of which I had not heard of, as well as some in England that would not be mine until Eleanor died.

Richard signed the document, as did I.

'Come along, let's follow the bishop,' he said.

I rose very carefully, making sure to keep my head steady and straight. Bishop Jean led us out of the crowded guard hall and down the steps of the castle yard, where we were met by the blinding heat of the late spring sunshine. He had before him the trumpeters, the singing boys, the crusader banners, and Richard's banner. Behind us were the banners of the noble lords, intent on reaching Jerusalem, but not before attending a good celebration. The square before the castle was now thronged with celebrants, musicians, singers, and locals looking for a festival.

Richard had not disappointed them. 'I've had wine and beer stalls set up,' he said. He also pointed out spit-roasting meats: mutton, pork and beef, filling the air with mouth-watering aromas. We were joined by Joan and our ladies.

'A wedding feast to rival that of Canaan before the wine ran out,' quipped Joan boldly.

'Is that heavy?' asked Alazne, looking at my crown and attracting the attention of Richard. He said something to one of his squires, and the lad dashed off. Soon we reached the harbour's edge and stopped to admire the view.

'How many ships are there now, Richard?' I asked, for the water was a forest of masts.

'Near one hundred have found their way here, but my finest have been diverted to Famagusta. We shall convene there soon. There are my war galleys with arms, armour and the best of my fighting men, who were scattered by the storm but who all rowed to safety diligently. I wish to preserve their strength. Then there are some more *hippagōga*, with more destriers. The Holy Lands will wilt before their might. As soon as Comnenus is in my grasp, we'll be off. The Saracens will not resist a full cavalry charge. And there are store ships packed with siege engines, too.'

Richard's squire came back. He was carrying a gold circlet, which he handed to the king.

'Will this do, my sweet? It's a lot lighter,' he said to me.

'Why, thank you, Richard. How thoughtful.'

'Not at all. I must look after my queen.'

Richard was extending greetings to one side and then the other. It was quite exhausting, but the smile on his face was genuine, as was the friendliness of those bold enough to come near. Eventually, we wound our way from the waterside to the king's pavilion. It wasn't much quieter inside; it was evident that some of his lords had been liberal with the wine, but our path to the top table was cleared. I was grateful to sit down and rest my aching feet.

'Oh, Mother of God,' mumbled Joan, 'more eager lords seeking our company.'

'Be nice, sister,' whispered Richard. 'They are working for God.' He stood and greeted the congregation. 'My queen and I bid you welcome. We invite you to enjoy the rest of the day.' Then he turned to Hugo. 'Have they found the Griffon jester yet?'

Hugo grinned. 'They have him penned in Kyrenia Castle, Your Highness. The news is just in.'

'Good, good. When will you be ready to move from Cyprus? I expect my war galleys to be at Famagusta by now.'

If enjoying our wedding feast was Richard's intent, he was not successful. Commanders and captains came up to the table for instructions or clarifications, while Mercadier hovered behind us all the time.

Then there was the endless presentation of meats, fruits, sweetmeats and wine. Richard asked that I call in my musicians, though dancing was still prohibited.

Joan comforted me. 'You can have an after-wedding feast with music and dancing when this war is over.'

'I suppose so. All these men are so loud; we need a court with women to calm them down.'

'True, but we stand alone in the midst of this carnival.'

I laughed. 'There must be women in Outremer. We surely aren't the only ones left south of Italy.'

'I've heard that there are women of all persuasions in the Holy Land, and that some cater for soldiers' needs.'

I was shocked. 'You mean…?'

'Sin, Berengaria, sin.'

'Holy Mother of God, how can that be?'

'It is the eternal fight against the nature of man, I'm afraid, always looking for somewhere to plant his seed.'

'And my new husband is no exception, I pray.'

'Except that you have God's blessing, Berengaria; make the most of it.'

'I intend to. How soon do you think we can leave?'

'Soon, I think. It is dark outside now, and I know that Richard is an early riser, always eager to deal with his duties. I'm afraid that you may well come second to Richard's responsibilities, Berengaria; he is a very focused man.'

We continued to converse for a while and watched as the wedding feast became ever more rowdy. Eventually, it became too tiring and Richard whispered, 'Do you think that we could leave now, my queen? I'm beginning to wilt in the heat. There's much to do, and we have some business to conduct between us.'

'Yes, Richard, I was thinking the same. Do you think that we could get out of here before those trumpeters notice?'

'I'll send them to the front of the pavilion and we'll disappear out the back. Our boudoir tent is not far away — in the olive orchard, well-guarded and quiet. Joan, walk down towards those trumpeters and send them out, then walk back here and leave with your ladies. We'll have left. Mercadier will walk with you.'

'What? Am I bait for your fish-eyed lords?'

'Yes. Distract them for me, please, just this once, Joan.'

With a sigh, Joan swayed towards the exit, closely followed by Mercadier and several dozen pairs of eyes.

I slipped out of my chair and out through the servants' entrance at the back. Richard caught hold of me and held me close. Then, hand in hand, we went out into the darkness of the orchard. The place was infested with Richard's personal guards.

'I thought we would be alone, Richard?'

He did not reply, but his grip on my hand tightened a little.

We arrived at his boudoir tent. It was encircled by burning braziers and soldiers just out of the light.

'Now we are alone. Well, as much as a king can be.' He held back the canvas door and I ducked inside. It was candlelit and sumptuously decorated with hangings and floor rugs. There were chairs, and behind some flimsy drapes was an enormous bed. In the middle was an incense burner, giving off delicate aromas.

'I've dismissed my squires,' he said. 'Do you want to have your tending ladies here to help you undress?'

'That will not be necessary, Richard, I'm sure that we can manage it between us, fumble through it, somehow. Are you shy?'

He reddened, common enough with people of his blond hair and freckles, but unknown by his reputation. I was surprised.

'Err, I have tumbled wenches before, but you, my sweet, are different. I have not known a princess ... queen. Jesu, yes, a queen. But one so small, how will we manage?'

I tittered, 'Very carefully, my lord, and gently.'

'Ho, ho. Here, undo these ties at the back for me.'

He bent down to allow me to reach the ties, then standing he flung off the long tunic.

'There, good, good,' he said, turning round to face me.

His hands trembled as he placed his hands on my shoulders and turned me to unlace my gown. When he was down to my hips his hands encircled me to hold my breasts, they seemed to shrink in his huge hands and a vision of something else too huge to manage flashed cross my mind.

I twisted back to look up at him, his face was almost out of sight.

'Dear me, dear Berri,' he muttered, 'hold tight.'

Picking me up and crossing the tent he stood me on a chair.

'There, we'll see what we have crowned now,' he said softly as he pulled the gown down over my hips to reveal my bush.

'Ah, it's been a while,' he whispered into my hair. I was responding and could feel desire building. I wondered how he intended to mount me.

As he picked me up my legs went around his back and I could feel my core touch his stomach as he strode back across to the bed and laid me gently down. Standing he pulled down his breeches and netherwear and was naked before me.

It was not standing, but sort of lolled from side to side as he stepped out of his clothes and knelt on the bed, straddling my hips.

'Well, Queen?'

'Well, King, you have me at your mercy,' I replied.

Leaning down he put his head close to mine and we enjoyed the first full kiss, our tongues now playing a part. It altered my perception, now I was abandoning myself to him and I was ready for it.

'Do I please you, Richard?'

'Yes, yes, I never want to see a straight line ever again.'

He grinned, a handsome, wicked, meaningful grin. Then, quick as anything, he lifted my legs and a shiver went through me.

I watched his eyes journey down to my mound.

His hands came round the back to cup my buttocks, squeezing and pulling me towards him, then gripping my shoulders and he was on top of me with his face nuzzling into my hair and I was lost in desire. Now I wanted to feel him inside me.

Looking up again he asked, 'Are you ready, my sweet?'

My arms encircled his neck and I searched out his lips again; they were gentle, his tongue exciting and the taste of him an invitation. We said nothing more but closing my hands behind his neck I let them briefly take my weight as I wrapped my legs around his back. With my buttocks cupped in his hands again and his fingers prying, he twisted us over and in an eye-blink I was straddled across him and it was he who was on his back.

'Don't want to squash you, Berri, take your time.'

Mother of mercy, pray for me.

Sitting still I watched as he kneaded my nipples and then, becoming bolder, my hands went behind my back to find his thing.

'Oh!' he murmured. He shivered when my hands touched flesh, different flesh … a man's privy flesh. I was doing it: the devil's tool in my hand.

'Jesu, Richard,' I responded, unthinking. It was soft and pliant. How was he going to insert that feeble thing?

'Ah!' he said, his eyes taking on an odd look. 'I can feel I'm not ready. Let us take some time, Berri, tis best to take a bit of time.'

His hands went around my neck and pulled my face on to his. Our tongues met and I felt his hands sliding along my thighs, his fingers moved to touched my lips and a thrill ran through my body from groin to head. I would not be satisfied, that I knew, until we were enjoined. Fingers stroked and explored, tongues tasted and my hardened nipples scratched at his chest.

'Are you ready?'

In answer I fell off him on to my back bending my knees, he formed a bridge over me with his great body and I felt him at my entry, long limbs supporting his weight.

I was scared he might fall on me, and then other things took my mind from that. Our breathing became as one as I felt him touch and begin to move, then he tried to insert it with his hands, it was at me and I gasped at the feel of it as I determined to take him in, wrapping my legs around his back and thrusting up. Then something altered and I heard him gasp.

'Jesu, no!' he cried and fell to one side, pulling a cover over his nether parts as he turned.

I was not to be denied, and pulling back down the cover I threw a leg over him. I heard sounds of frustration as he put his hands over his face and with a taut voice cried, 'No, no.'

He was breathing heavily as I squirmed on top of him, but there was no response from his body. I pushed up on my arms and looked down. It was hardly there, he was not responding. I looked at his face and whispered, 'Richard.'

Opening his hands he stuttered, 'I'm sorry.' He closed his eyes.

I wondered what he apologised for. Something was missing, not quite there.

'What do you mean, Richard?'

His eyes opened again. 'I thought of the Lord, the holy city, went off ahead, too much to think about, yes, yes. Don't ye think?'

'No, I have no experience. Does my body not please you?'

'It does, I've never seen better. D'ye not see, this chastity thing, it sort of puts things off. Do you want to try again?'

I sat up, legs wide open across his hips, I was very wet and felt behind me, but he was still soft.

I took his question as an invitation. I'd not had a man to explore before and here was one and my curiosity was fully awakened. I had made no vows of chastity.

By now I knew that he would not hurt me, and set to exploring him and his strange manhood, the balls hard to the touch but the soft finger-like thing flopping about in my hand.

He gave a weak smile and placed his hands upon my shoulders.

'You'll give me another chance later, yes?'

'Several, if you wish,' I grinned back. 'What does this feel like?' I would not give up and my curious hands continued to explore, then at last a result and he had, it seemed, to have rid himself of his doubts and some strength began to flow into his thing, but then there was a commotion outside, someone shouting.

'You cannot! The king is occupied.'

'I must, I'm under strict instructions.'

'What's this?'

I recognised Mercadier's voice, angry.

'Who sent you?'

'The captain of the harbour guard, the king must be told.'

I cursed the canvas walls; they were not as privy as I had assumed.

Richard's thing suddenly disappeared from my hand as he sat up.

'I'm sorry, it must be my galleys, or worse, enemy ships. Can you slip off, Berri?'

I lifted over a leg and sat on the bed, watching him as he began to dress.

'Dog's bollocks, someone will pay for this, yes, yes.'

He turned around and drew up his small breeches. I had a last look at his dangling bits before he shouted, 'Squires!' Then, grabbing the covers he helped to draw the sheet over me. 'Sorry about this, I need their help to get meself armoured, tis a bit complicated, what, what.'

He went to the curtain and drawing it across, said, 'I'll send for your ladies, must see what's ado on the water.'

Blowing a kiss he closed the flimsy curtain as his squires came bursting into the tent.

'Dress me and be quick about it,' he commanded.

They were, and I was left sitting on the bed watching my king being dressed through a gauze curtain in the dim guttering candlelight.

Oh well, Berri, so that's a wedding night, is it? I thought it might have lasted a bit longer; serves you right for marrying in the middle of a war. A queen but not a wife. One comes with the other, does it not? Where are my ladies? Then I pulled a pillow over my head to wet the linen with my tears.

A NOTE TO THE READER

Dear Reader,

I would be very grateful if you manage to find time to leave a review on **Amazon** or **Goodreads**. Reviews are the author's lifeblood.

More details about my writing can be found on my website:

www.history-reimagined.co.uk

Thank you.

Austin Hernon

Sapere Books is an exciting new publisher of brilliant fiction and popular history.

To find out more about our latest releases and our monthly bargain books visit our website: **saperebooks.com**

Printed in Great Britain
by Amazon